THE GENTLE DEGENERATES

As she sat there, she was doing a little dance, a dance that would be unseen by anyone who wasn't paying the closest attention. Her tongue would flick out from time to time and lick the portion of her lips just at the line which divided the inside of her mouth from the outside. Her hands fluttered back and forth from her lap to her hair, and her fingers spun an invisible fabric over her, a transparent shawl which she kept removing in order to expose her ripe breasts, which sagged and pressed against the tight shirt she wore. Each shift of her torso sent her tits shuddering against the cloth and outlined her nipples more sharply. My eyes went to her chest to watch the soft mounds move like seaweed in the tide, lolling lazily back and forth, screaming for my hand to reach out and grab them gingerly, as though plucking a ripe pear from a tree. And most of all I became aware of how she moved on her chair: a continual squirming shuffle with her ass that must have come near to searing her panties. Although there was hardly an external movement, she continued to squeeze her thighs together and let them fall open.

THE
GENTLE
DEGENERATES

Marco Vassi

A Nexus Book
published by
the Paperback Division of
W. H. Allen & Co Plc

A Nexus Book
Published in 1989
by the Paperback Division of
W. H. Allen & Co Plc
Sekforde House, 175–9 St John Street,
London W1V 4LL

Printed in Great Britain by
Cox & Wyman Ltd, Reading

ISBN 0 352 32428 7

For Rennie
Who helped me feel the pain

Would it have been worthwhile,
To have bitten off the matter with a smile,
To have squeezed the universe into a ball
To roll it towards some overwhelming question,
To say: 'I am Lazarus, come back from the dead,
Come back to tell you all, I shall tell you all' –
If one, settling a pillow by her head,
Should say: 'That is not what I meant at all.
That is not it, at all.'

From *'The Love Song of J. Alfred Prufrock'*
by T. S. ELIOT

Intimacy is as frightening as freedom
Richard Fichtel

THE
GENTLE
DEGENERATES

(1)

THERE IS LOVE, which is neither personal nor impersonal; and there is sex, which is either personal or impersonal. We love, and want to fuck. But we fuck, and so often love disappears. The activity of sex is not difficult to come to terms with. We understand our bodies, we learn how to let go, we strive for pleasure, and learn how to give-to-get. The Indians catalogued the positions and the techniques many thousands of years ago, and the Tibetans made Tantric Yoga, the yoga of sex, into a vehicle for enlightenment. A few millennia and half a world away, scientists of the West have measured heart rate, blood pressure, and changes in colour of the asshole during the sexual act.

But this is all descriptive, even statistical. The problem is in the *nature* of sex, its essential quality. And how does it relate to this very difficult problem of living together, of making a marriage, with its traps of staleness and jealousy, its pitfalls of hidden hostility and of compromises which erode the integrity of both partners?

The story begins one winter afternoon at Kennedy Airport. The plane taking Regina back to California had just left the ground, winging into the grey sky, and suspicion set in. It bit into my stomach and filled my mind with acrid fantasies, hateful visions of betrayal and diabolical control. Within minutes after her departure, she ceased being a person to me, and become a force, an influence on my life. The games we played were tolerable and even exciting when we were together, but apart, they seemed grotesque. And in the face of them, I had promised to join her within a month in Mendocino, where we were to buy a house and begin a life together.

I got into my car and drove back to the city, the sleet beating at the window with a rampant chatter. Winter was visiting its usual punishment on the city, tearing at the streets and bleak buildings with vicious winds. It suited my mood perfectly. As I drove, I noticed that the caked blood at the root of the nail on my middle finger was turning brown. It was just a few hours ago that she had lain in my bed, her cunt hot and wet from excitement and the flow of her period. We both knew that she would be leaving in a few hours; we both realised that we might not be seeing one another again, despite the fervid promises, despite the exchange of rings, despite the aching need we had for one another.

We fucked as though it were the last time. I wanted to swallow her whole, to possess her fully and finally, and simultaneously to destroy her, to make it impossible for her ever to do this with anyone else. When I slid my finger past the dry lips and met the slightly moist bud which opened to her inner cunt, it was both a caress and an intrusion. My eyes flicked to hers and a look of total calculation passed between us. Deep within her a subtle change took place, a shift in mood to counter what I was feeling. I could read the message. She would let me fuck her, but I wouldn't be getting any more than her flesh. Her emotions and thoughts would stay guarded. I had a sudden impulse to kick her out of the bed and let her go begging, but my cock was already hard and, as usual, it overrode all intelligent strategy in favour of the immediate tactic.

I acquiesced to the ploy and withdrew behind mechanical activity. I rubbed my finger in and out of the now moist slit until I knew she was minimally prepared for entrance. Without any grace, I hoisted my body over hers and placed the tip of my cock against her cunt lips, and slowly entered her resentful box.

There was no warmth to her, just a clammy

acceptance. I pushed all the way in and received a small response, a physical reflex any cunt would make when a cock entered, no matter how detached the woman was. I began to feel the solidity of her, and I slid my hands down her back to cup her ass and pull it toward me. She moved slightly, adjusting the angle of penetration, and I flushed with the melting and yearning sensations that fill me whenever I fuck; but this time I refused to go with them. Too often I had been the detonator which blasted her out of indifference, bringing her to a climax, and been left hanging after her orgasm. Now I concentrated all my sensation in my cock, and got into an impersonal ride where the only thing that mattered was friction. Heat bubbled in my balls, and I began to buck into her, slamming my pubic bone into her pelvis. It was the time when I would normally hang loose, waiting for her to find the rhythm so we could dig it together. But now I just took off on my own trip, and the excitement of it spread to her thighs. Her legs went up and she dug into my shoulders with her nails. Her mouth slackened, and tiny moans fluttered in her throat. She rolled her ass under and lifted her pelvis beneath me so that her cunt opened deeper to the thrusts. But just as she began to get into the motion of it, I began to come. I let everything go and felt the ripples sweep up and down my body, making my legs tremble and my spine waver. My head snapped

back and I cried out as a full load of sperm splashed from my cock into her waiting pussy.

I sank down on top of her, and a small sigh of
disappointment escaped her lips. I smiled to
myself. If she wanted to play tight-asshole while
we were fucking, I would match her moves and
win. And just as I thought that, a deep cloud of
sadness passed over me. What was I doing? This
was Regina, the woman closest to me in the world.
Why were we playing these spiteful games?

I had known her for two years. We met on the
Coast and lived together, on and off, half a dozen
times. Both of us had been married, and done
enough live-ins to be wary of all the traps of marriage, of any bonded relationship. We were also
consummate game players, and loved to have an
audience. In fact, we were never so much together
as when we operated as a team in the face of
others. Very early I learned that, unless we were
careful, we could use each other up in short order,
and drop the relationship to go look for other
scenes. And we were both tired of shopping. The
desire for security and intimacy is subtle and
strong. The animal that I still am wants a solitary
mate, faithful to me alone, which no other male
can plunder. When I suck Regina's nipple into my
mouth and savage her breast with my teeth, I
see her face melt, from the tense lines of the
independent thirty-year-old, the self-sufficient
school teacher, the mother of a small boy, to the

soft, open lines of a gasping teenage girl reaching for her first kiss. Then all the liberated notions of my political training fade at once, and a single primeval cry rises in my breast – 'This is mine!' And that is what feels right, the possession, the access. I want no one else ever to know that moment of heart-tearing bliss when all the beauty that is Regina bursts forth, as her lips open and her mouth invites my mouth, as her cunt goes soft and yearns for my cock, as she rolls her head from side to side in a kind of gentle refusal-which-accepts, a refusal of the joy and ecstatic flow now coursing through her limbs and sending cascades of images crashing through her mind.

It is that more than anything which arouses me, which drives me to heights of mad lovemaking and need. Within her is an eternal 'no', an unchanging centre, forever virginal, which always tempts and asks to be won over. Perhaps that is what woman is, but with Regina, who understands herself so well, that constant denial lives at the surface, at the edge of her movement and talk. This is the *persona* she projects, that of a cockteasing bitch, and inside the woman cries for liberation from herself.

I have the key to her inside, and the key burns around my neck as it dangles from a chain of experience. It is like some medieval drama, and perhaps it is, for no matter how sophisticated I have become, I have not lost the fires of my genes and the scars of my history. I descend from the

Italians, and in my childhood learned of the world through the eyes of priests and feudal barons, now disguising themselves in twentieth-century suits on the streets of New York. My entire attitude toward women was formed in a place where women ranked little better than servants. And Regina is my lady, complete with chastity belt, a pan-frigidity to keep out other men when I am not with her.

She knows this and smiles about it. Part of her enjoys the game, so long as it remains a game that does not threaten to overwhelm the entire relationship. And it pleases me, until she begins to play her half of the scenario, taunting me with hints and half-smiles of adventures she might have had during my absence. Often I come home ready to fling open the door and find her in someone else's arms. I keep my schedule flexible so she can't be sure of my comings and goings. When I arrive I look into her eyes and at how she walks. I kiss her experimentally. I smell her hair. From these tests I can tell what the percentage of assurance is that she has not betrayed me. As she goes about her things, preparing dinner or reading or telephoning a friend, my eyes burn through her pants to feel into her ass, her cunt, to caress and probe all the skin of her thighs and breasts, psychically sniffing, licking, looking for clues. She retaliates by provoking me, sending me double signals. Before long the air is charged with excitement and lust. Then the tension breaks, and we find ourselves standing, gazing at one another, faces open, tongues moving, hips grinding subtly, eyes flashing. And then we are in one another's arms.

But it is more complex than simple jealousy, for I know that she is largely faithful to me. It is I who desire more. I also want her to be totally wanton, to pick men up on the street, to bring them home and there to strip and spread her legs on the bed, offer her juicy throbbing cunt to them. I want her to be without limits, to plunge into all the degradations, to swim in them. I want her to be a whore, with all the sluttishness and brash honesty of a whore. I want Regina to be free. And I know that in our civilisation sexual freedom comes to a person only when he or she has tasted deep of licentiousness. Only in this Pilgrim's Progress through the Perversions is it possible for a human being in our time to emerge into full actualisation.

I swing back and forth between the opposing needs. Two nights before she left, we fought. It was one of those cold knife-edge arguments that has neither tears nor rage, nor the honest clash of physical violence. And as I became worn down by it, feeling my defences crumble and the sense of aloneness rising inside me, she saw the manhood waning and struck with her strongest weapon. 'I feel wild,' she said. 'I feel like a wild nymph.' I looked at her bleakly. She went on. 'When I feel this way is when I have adventures. I remember once I was fighting with a lover who said I couldn't satisfy him sexually. I walked out and went folk-dancing. I met Dan. He didn't say a word, he just nodded at me and I followed him out to his motorcycle. He took me to his place and fucked me all night long. I enjoyed it completely and my cunt was sore for two days afterwards. There wasn't anything wrong with me.'

I heard the words and they were like razor cuts inside. Excitement at her wantonness burned through my need to have her pure. I collapsed and felt as though I were coming to a panic-filled dead end. I lay down and curled into the foetal position, nursing my hurt. Regina flashed the scene immediately, and without missing a beat changed from White Goddess to Earth Mother. She came over and put my head in her lap, and stroked me until I filled with warmth and gratitude. My eyes became moist even though I realized that she was playing carrot-and-stick with me. I fell asleep like that, resting on her thighs.

Later we got up and went to Brooklyn Heights for Syrian food. We strolled on the Esplanade and watched Manhattan doing its night-time scene across the river, growling in power and speed, ablaze with light. It got very romantic and it was like first love all over again, holding hands and holding one another tightly. We went home in a cloud of euphoria and headed straight for bed.

We took off our clothes and moved into one another's arms without a hesitation. I was bubbling over and she moved with a joyful, steady beat. She lay back, her ass in my hands, pumping her cunt into my cock, and I melted into delirium and spasms of sweet melancholy. This was *us* fucking, Regina and I, and she was giving me her all. I possessed her as she wanted me to, and I alone received the centre of her love.

Yet running counterpoint to all the pleasure was the thought, 'Only because you copped to her game, and only because she continued to find you accessible. If she had gone out by herself for dinner, might she not have met another man, a man with glowing eyes and hot hands, a man who could see the little girl inside and offer her a proper lollipop? Once she had said to me, 'I'm a sucker for anyone who sweet-talks me,' and again, 'I let him fuck me because he told me I was beautiful at a time when I had forgotten I could be beautiful.'

The fantasy took hold. I saw her now, still fucking, biting her lips in passion, her hands fluttering a tattoo like pigeons' wings along the man's back. Yet the man wasn't me. It was any man who happened to fill this particular slot at this particular time. I looked down at her. Her eyes were closed. Her lean dancer's body rippled and writhed under me, as she sucked at my cock with her now sloshing cunt, and put her legs around my thighs in that most intimate of all embraces. Her entire ripe body began to open, and I wasn't sure it was me she was opening to. There was just man, just the male, only the cock.

Torment burned through me as the sensations of sex forced me to move. I lost my breath and my ribcage became sore. I cried out, 'Regina,' and yearned for her to respond to me. But all I received was an impersonal caress. 'Don't stop,' she said.

I bounced immediately from sorrow to anger. The bitch! She was betraying me while she was in my very arms by nullifying me, making me a stud to rub herself on. I was past all notions of reason or logic. There was pure feeling, and the thoughts which that feeling fed. She was worse than a whore, for a whore makes no pretence of sharing, while the slut lying under me wooed me with promises of love and fidelity. Now she seemed filthy, and all my hidden hatred of women burst through and flooded the experience of sex. All she wanted was a male animal.

And so I became that animal. From inside me growls rumbled up and through my teeth. I hunched my back and pinned her down, as though I were a great cat about to slash the throat of a deer. I bit into her flesh, nipping at her jaw and shoulders and chest. She bucked and dug her claws into my back. Pain matched pain. She opened her eyes in confusion, and for a full second she didn't recognise me. She floundered in her responses and I screwed up my eyes to smile wickedly into her face. She saw that she had been caught and two rays of hatred shot back at me. I laughed in exultation and slapped her across the mouth. She screamed in anger. 'Fuck you, fuck you, I'll kill you!' she cried.

I yelled at the top of my lungs, a crackling jungle cry that drove her head back into the pillow. Then, very softly, I said, 'You stupid little liar.' And with that, drove my cock into her as hard as I could. A wavering cry fluttered up from her chest and she brought her hands to her mouth, making soft unclenched fists. Her legs came up and opened my cock into her like a man swimming in a deep lake. Her gaping, brimming pussy took every shock and thrust and got hotter and hotter. I slammed into her like a stallion rearing against his first bit, and she moaned, over and over again, 'Oh no, don't, yes, do it, no, please, oh, help me, fuck me, fuck me.'

By now there was no personality left. It was sheer energy, and I looked down to see her quivering breasts, jiggling with each movement, her belly all wrinkled from being folded over, and her ass like a deep steaming dish on which was offered the unquenchable cunt. The heat flashes began to break up and down my body, and I urged her to let it all go, whispering, 'Come on. come on, do it, reach for it.' Her cunt rose up like a fish leaping from the water and swallowed my cock whole. My bowels fell out, my eyes rolled back, and, like an epileptic in full fit, I felt my spine go into great rolling convulsions as I shot a thick volley into her begging crack.

And then it was over. Almost immediately.

There was none of that mutual settling into silence that follows a good fuck, I tasted only the bitterness of those who overextend their energy in fucking a fantasy while forgetting the person who is the source of the act. It was an impersonal fuck, a theatrical bang, the kind I can enjoy with tricks I pick up at parties, but which I cannot dig with Regina. For a moment I hovered at the edge of once and for all, making her impersonal to me, killing the myth of specialness with which she had infected me and which I nurtured. I wanted then to treat her like any one of the hundreds of men and women I have known and fucked. Why should I make this particular human being into a fetish? Why can't she be just a good piece of ass in bed? Why did I come to insist on exclusiveness, with all its concurrent jealousy and limiting of consciousness?

I wanted very much to get up and leave, never to see her again. I had no feelings but disgust and self-hatred. Yet, when I looked at her, I suddenly wanted to let go and just sink into her arms, to heal the split between us which burned like acid on my skin. We stared at each other over an immense distance, while eddies of love and hate, of trust and insecurity, flickered around the edges of our eyes. For no good reason, I smiled, and she grimaced and turned her face away. I pulled back from her and my now limp cock slithered out of the already cold cunt hole.

I rolled over on my back and we lay silent for

a few minutes, then she said, 'Do you have the cigarettes by you?' And that was the making of the compact, the closing of the deed. It was the signal that we had not brought it off, but could now talk about it, talk about fucking, about love, about the future, about the state of civilisation, about anything in the world, because we were too tense to lie quietly and watch the universe float by.

I got the cigarettes and we lit them slowly, watching each other's eyes over the flame. She lay back then, sprawled out to stare at the ceiling. I remained propped on one elbow, and looked at her body. The smallish breasts which had seemed boyishly exciting now looked merely inadequate. Her cunt hair was matted with sperm and blood. Her toenails were ragged and her mouth had reformed into a thin mean slit. Everything about her which had turned me on a few moments earlier now seemed slightly repulsive.

When I was younger, I was devastated by such changes in mood, and would have been angry at myself or hated the woman. But now I realised that was the way of things, that when passion did not flow free and unencumbered, but became embroiled in distorting fantasies, then beauty became ugliness and the delicious juices of the body tasted rank and stale and rotten. We smoked for a long time.

Then she turned to me. 'What was that all about?' she asked.

'Weren't you there?' I asked, not without an edge.

'I was someplace,' she said. 'Not the same place you were.'

Already it was beginning. The rationalisations would dim the sharp glare of the situation. This moment, enacted between millions of men and women, could be handled with anger or bitterness, but with us the liberal mode was most congenial. We reasoned that neither of us was 'doing' anything to the other; there was no blame. Rather, she was in one place and I was in another, and there is no way to make judgements about what we did. There was no better or worse; only different. My mind accepted the logic of the scheme, but my blood boiled against it.

'You don't want to give,' I said very loudly. 'And that's all right. You can keep your precious cunt locked up tight. But don't expect me to keep coaxing you and coming after you. Try finding someone else with as much patience as I have putting up with all your shit.'

'*My shit*!' she yelled, picking up the ball on one bounce. And then we were off to another round. 'If you weren't so uncertain and spineless,' she continued, 'I would have enough security to let go with you.'

It could have gone on for some time, but we were both tired, and it ended as all our arguments end, in a feeling of sheepishness. The deed was done, and there was no going back to erase or change anything. The only direction was forward, probably to more of the same.

We lit two more cigarettes to bring the chapter to a close. Another storm had been weathered, another notch of insight had been noted in the log, and we looked at one another like two warriors whose closeness lies in their mutual inability to totally do each other in. And in that look there was an odd tenderness which is the special mark of how I feel about her.

For a long minute we moved into one another's eyes. Our mutual projections joined: she saw in me the me that is most me-for-her, and I saw in her the her that is most her-for-me. And the selves we saw in one another saw one another's selves, and the jagged vibration which had just set our teeth on edge found its proper groove, and we were back home with each other.

I put my cigarette out and laid my head down on her belly; I put my hands under her and felt her full, tough ass cheeks in my hands. Her body seemed to call me into it, and I began moving down toward her crotch, to put my mouth on her cunt, to lick those delicate lips and kiss what had again become a sheer dear fragrance.

But she put her hand down and pushed my face away. It was done gently and tenderly, but the message was clear: 'Get away from my cunt.' For a split second I felt the old anger, but I was too weary to give it rein. I let it pass and contented

28

myself with getting up and asking with a false heartiness, 'Want some coffee?'

'I'd love some,' she said, smiling. I plunged one last time behind her eyes, to see if there was the slightest indication that she would cop to what had just happened. But either she was unconscious of her behaviour and motives, or else an absolute master at whisking away what she didn't want seen. There was nothing to do about it, so I put the matter out of my mind and went into the kitchen to boil some water.

BEFORE SHE LEFT, we decided to try living together in California. There is something about the aura of such a decision that obscures all the real difficulties and impossibilities. I thought that, with enough will and constancy, it might be possible to resolve our problems, to dissolve them in time. I had some business to finish up, so I intended to join her in a month. We bought rings and made promises of fidelity.

Now it was Sunday morning, and she had been gone a week. Two nights ago, she called, and it was one of those long distance long-distance conversations, where the words become a meaningless electronic jumble and the person is far away. We had little to talk about except our respective gossip, and even that only served as a vehicle for shunting resentments, for paying off old debts, real and imaginary. Without even the warmth of her presence to offset the negative feelings, I sensed all the tightness in her.

Apropos of nothing, she mentioned a male friend who had visited her house. She described him in some detail and I wondered what she was getting at. 'He wanted to make me, she said. There was a long pause during which I felt the familiar burning beginning in my stomach. She continued, 'But I showed him the ring and told him all about us.' I waited for the rest of it, waited for her to say that he didn't turn her on, that since she was away from me only a few days, she couldn't even think of another man. But the opposite followed. 'The only thing that stopped me,' she said, 'was that I knew you would be jealous.' I couldn't resist the bait. 'What happened?' I asked. 'Oh, we talked,' she said, 'and it was very friendly. I told him he could come by to visit any time he wanted.' The taunting in her voice was unmistakable; she was telling me that I had better get there as soon as possible, or else.

I didn't respond, and the rest of the conversation dribbled off into inanities. When I hung up I felt furious and sick. The barb had lodged home, and now I would be living with the spectre of this faceless, nameless man hanging around the edges of her life, in that amorphous California style, where people act more like sludges than human beings, and attach themselves to vortices of energy, waiting for the crumbs to fall, as fall they will. I pictured him in the living room, prowling, while Regina lay upstairs with her supply of dope and her beckoning stare, lolling on the bed and fingering her cunt, deciding whether or not she will let this one have her, tossing up her desire for a fuck to see if it came down heads or tails.

And worse than that was my reaction, my stupid jealous response, instead of the thing I wanted to say, which is, 'Go ahead, fuck whoever you like. See if they will put up with your temperamental pussy for long. Find some inarticulate pothead who will rub you with his tool. But when you want someone who knows what it's all about, who knows how you like to be touched, who knows all the ways you try to hide and is able to come find you, then give me a call. But by that time, bitch, I might be too busy.'

Yet some weakness was holding me down, making me feeble. Some great neurotic hand had me by the balls and was forcing me to play the role of spineless fool, copping to her taunts and allowing myself to fall into impotent rages. Compounding it was the fact that I didn't have a clean conscience myself, because the night before I had gone to visit Joan, and spent the evening fucking.

It had started innocently enough. We had been friends for a long time, and for one reason or another had never got down to making it. We fell into that kind of coy chumminess that women put on with men whom they don't want to fuck, but don't discourage either. It's a way of keeping the lines of access open. When I knocked at her door there was no idea of sex in my mind. I wanted some music and a little dope. More than anything, I needed a Vicks rub for my soul.

She was in the middle of ironing clothes, and I prepared to make my visit a short one. But before I knew it, she stopped what she was doing and sat down next to me, paying unusually close attention to my rap. Some subtle change in the vibrations caught me up, and I switched my set from verbal cues to body language, that means of communication that tells most directly where we are at, but which we ignore most of the time.

Immediately everything slowed down, and the speed train of talk began to make stops to allow the passengers to look at the scenery. Which in this case was captivating. Joan was small in that way which suggests tight pussy and hard nipples. The fact that she was perfectly proportioned made her size all the more delicious. We fell into a lilting talk about movies we had seen, a topic which allowed us to speak mechanically and thus free our eyes and ears for more meaningful exchanges.

As she sat there, she was doing a little dance, a dance that would be unseen by anyone who wasn't paying the closest attention. Her tongue would flick out from time to time and lick the portion of her lips just at the line which divided the inside of her mouth from the outside. It was like a tiny hand coming to the edge of a cave and inviting me in. But the cave was a full, wet, continually sensitive mouth, which now seemed to be calling for a tongue or cock to visit it. Her hands fluttered back and forth from her lap to her hair, and her fingers spun an invisible fabric over her, a transparent shawl which she kept removing in order to expose her ripe breasts, which sagged and pressed against the tight shirt she wore. Each shift of her torso sent her tits shuddering against the cloth and outlined her nipples more sharply. My eyes went to her chest to watch the soft mounds move like seaweed in the tide, lolling lazily back and forth, screaming for my hand to reach out and grab them gingerly, as though plucking a ripe pear from a tree. And most of all I became aware of how she moved on her chair: a continual squirming shuffle with her ass that must have come near to searing her panties. Although there was hardly any external movement, she continued to squeeze her thighs together and let them fall open.

By this time I was breathing rapidly and deeply. The words we were speaking dropped between us and went unheard and uncared-about. I leaned forward and watched her face as she spoke. Everything about her was alive, the small twitches of her mouth, and the way her eyes kept thrusting and yielding like the point of a fine fencing blade. Suddenly I saw her whole, this vibrant breathing creature of sound and touch, her entire body a field of pleasure and pain, and ripping aside all the silly conventions of time and place, I found myself in eternity with her, with no other considerations or connections, with not a thought for other people or other ties. Regina became phantasmagorical. This was now, this was real. There was no other context within which to dig it. Joan flashed it at the same time, and without a flicker of hesitation we moved into each other's space and our lips met in that most electrifying of all experiences, the first kiss.

For a few minutes there was nothing but the tentativeness of touch. My hands roamed her entire body, finding out the answers to all the questions I had asked myself during the years I could see her but did not feel her; how firm her ass was, and how sensitive her nipples, and did the little bulge above her belly button mean that she was totally relaxed into her womb? For if she was, then fucking her would be different from fucking most women. It would mean being able to dive deep into her cunt, past the surface excitement of her lips and clitoris, and thrash about in a welcoming, wallowing vagina that could feel my cock and grip at it and come around it with heavy ripples and an overflow of hot juice.

We separated and looked at one another in that classic instant of dislocation halfway between the oblivion of passion and the guidelines of social reality. 'Are you sure you want to fuck me?' she said. 'I wouldn't want it to make us stop being friends.' I understood what she meant and hastened to reassure her. 'There are people I fuck who aren't my friends, and there are friends whom I don't fuck; but best in the world are fucking buddies.' She smiled at that. 'Why don't you wait for me in the bedroom?' she said. 'I have to go to the john first.'

I walked off to the bedroom and was surprised to find myself swaggering. It wasn't with any sense of conquest or John Wayneliness. Just a simple zoological response to the situation.

I took off all my clothes except my shirt. It occurred to me that it would be indelicate to be lying there bare-assed naked as she came into the room. I am always surprising myself by finding odd bits and pieces of a conservative sexual psyche knocking around my consciousness. It reminded me of the time I lost my virginity in a San Francisco whorehouse. As I had waited in the room for the chick to show, I decided to keep my pants and socks on, but removed my shoes and shirt. And then wondered whether smoking a cigarette would give me bad breath and whether she would mind that. Actually, when she arrived, she just pulled out my cock to check for clap and then upped the price ten dollars by offering to give me head.

Joan came in, still fully dressed. We looked at each other, and a great self-consciousness filled the room. Theoretically, we were inflamed with passion, or at least that was supposed to be the reason men and women fucked. But actually all I felt was a kind of disinterested curiosity, wondering how she tasted and smelled, and whether she would dive all the way in at once or had some restraining notions about modesty. She climbed onto the bed and put her arms around me. 'I want you to know that this isn't just fucking for me,' she said. 'I'm doing this because I really like you. Do you like me?'

'Sure, I like you,' I said, and it was true. It was a little annoying to have to give a verbal assurance, however. It had been a while since I went to bed with anyone I couldn't talk with, or whose head I didn't dig. All of the sexual games, including debauchery, were infinitely richer if shared with a person of equal intelligence, warmth, and humour.

Up to that moment, I hadn't even had an erection. She looked at me. 'I hope I'm enough for you,' she said. 'You're much more experienced than I am.' She was fresh and honest and that saved her naivete from mawkishness. Suddenly I felt very much like the impresario auditioning a bright young talent. 'Here, let me take your clothes off,' I said.

And solemnly, carefully, I removed all her clothing. First the shirt up over her head, revealing the pendulous breasts. They swung from side to side with the motion of her arms, and I leaned forward to tenderly take one nipple between my teeth and gently bite. I felt no response. Clearly

40

she wasn't breast sensitive yet. Then I let her skirt drop, and pushing her back on the bed, pulled her panties all the way down her legs. She brought her knees together and clamped her thighs shut in a pose of modesty and reserve. She was so obviously inviting plunder at the same time she was pulling away that it became an inflammatory posture.

Up to now the whole thing had had a sense of unreality about it, as though we were on stage performing the sex scene in someone else's script. I had had enough of that, and lay down next to her; I closed my eyes and moved into her arms.

From then on it was all magic and flow. All the months and years of knowing one another, and our bodies straining toward each other, broke through the restraint and we surged forward and inward. I grabbed her breasts in my hands and squeezed until I thought she would scream, but on her face there was just a look of untended desire. I kneaded her tits like dough, feeling the fullness of them, the succulent tension of their hang and stretch, massaging the rich complexity of flesh. I brought the nipples to my mouth and raked them with my teeth. She became all hands, running her fingers over me, feeling and rubbing every part of my body. She slid down and took my cock in her hands, and began squeezing it as though she couldn't feel it enough. I reached down and cupped her ass, pinching the soft flesh and spreading the cheeks apart, exposing her asshole and then running my fingers down the crack.

The heavy smell of cunt-saliva filled my nostrils and I moved one finger into her slit to see if she were as wet as she seemed. Already the slimy lubrication was coating the pink lips and dribbling out of the bottom to roll between her white thighs. I slid my left hand under her ass and brought my right hand from above, and entered her cunt from two different directions. She wriggled like a worm impaled on a fishhook. her mouth opened as though to let out a cry, but no sound emerged. I covered it with my own mouth, and was immediately drawn into the world of tongue and breath. She sucked at me as though she were hungry and thirsty. She licked my lips with her tongue and made soft moaning sounds into my throat. All the while she wriggled her torso and pushed her cunt deeper onto my fingers.

I leaned all my weight over her and she fell back deeper into the soft mattress, letting herself go slack. She seemed immensely vulnerable, and that inflamed me into wanting to crush her, to grind myself into her. I tightened my grip on her cunt and her mouth opened even wider, her arms went out at her sides and she moved her head back and forth as though saying 'no' very slowly. I came up unobtrusively, bringing my knees to her hips, and then, drawing my fingers out of her pussy, climbed up until I was kneeling by her head. My cock poked straight out and throbbed slightly; it came up over her mouth and eyes so that she became crosseyed in staring at it. Then, openly, looking her full in the face, I reared back and up and brought the tip of my rod right to her still-open lips. To my surprise, she brought her hands up and covered her eyes with her forearms. I leaned forward and lowered my organ into her waiting mouth.

She took it with a grunt. Suddenly she became all animal. She made low inarticulate sounds and lapped at my cock like a dog licking water. She gulped the entire length of it down, the base stretching her lips wide. The tip lodged in her throat and I sank deep into the wet warmth of her totally open mouth; I pumped my pelvis into her mouth as though it were a cunt, prodding and shifting and driving hard down into the core of her. Her legs came up and she brought her fingers up to my balls, making mock feeble efforts to push me away, and then pulling me even more into her. She grabbed my cock with her hands and jerked it against her tongue, hitting at it with her smacking lips. I watched her go deeper and deeper into her mindless cocksucking, and when she was completely exposed in total, wanton, gulping acceptance, I began to fuck her in the mouth as hard as I could. She flung back her arms and let everything hang out. She was ready to take whatever I wanted to do to her.

I brought my cock out slowly, and let it hang half an inch over her face. She reached up her tongue and said, 'Fuck me, fuck me in the mouth, fuck my mouth.' I brought my hand down and put my fingers into the sucking hole. She latched on to them with a deep suction, licking wildly, all the while staring into my eyes, watching me, letting herself be seen.

Suddenly a double fantasy invaded us. The stories she had heard as a child came to life in her mind, tales of girls who came to want the men who brutalised them, who became willing slaves. And now she was one of those women, having been called in naked to the suite of such a monster, lying amid his dope and music and books and metaphysical dreams of world empire. And he was treating her like a rag to wipe himself on, degrading her, and to her amazement and horror, she was loving it, wanting him to be harder, crueller. I saw myself burst into flames as I became pure Satan, black and violet, great horns sprouting from my head. I flicked my pointed tail, and hunched my haunches over her. The vision seared her brain, and the woman in her emerged wild-eyed and wonderful. Now she was moving turbulent body, living vibrant cunt, yearning breasts, wanting me, wanting my cock, wanting the man, the man, no matter how terrible he was, for the implacable cock lodged itself into her deepest cunt and held her in thrall.

I moved my body down slowly until I was stretched out over her, and then lowered my cock between her legs. I slid it down so that it passed her cunt and rubbed between her ass cheeks. She made little sobbing sounds and pressed her thighs tightly together. For a few minutes I continued to move into that warm fleshy space, made wet and slippery by the cunt secretions which oozed down from her hungry twat. Then I felt her bringing her pelvis back trying to get her cunt low enough to grab my cock, but I teased her with it, keeping it out of reach, far back. She began to grow frantic. Her nails dug into my shoulders and her body wriggled wildly. 'Please,' she said. 'Please.' I was adamant, and only drove deeper between her luscious buttocks, nudging at the tight asshole. Her forehead formed into a frown. 'I have to have it,' she said. 'Please give it to me. Fuck me, please.'

I raised my cock a half-inch and she bucked up gratefully, grabbing the head of it with her cunt lips. The moment it entered she relaxed, and with a long sigh let it slip slowly into her box. For me it was electrifying. It was the softest cunt I could remember, totally sensitive and responsive. Immediately, I lost all sense of differentiation between cock and cunt, and we became a single organism joined at the one organ, the cockcunt.

And then we began to move. Her cycles were perfectly attuned to mine. As I rode a particular wave and started to get hot behind it, she would rise to meet me, and we would take it together until something in our minds coalesced and we came to a kind of mental climax; then a few moments rest, and another wave would come by. It was like surfboarding, catching wave after wave, riding in to shore and paddling out for the next one, knowing that one of them would be the really big one to carry us singing home.

She suddenly changed her rhythm and began pushing hard against me. I resisted at first, and we rolled back and forth on the bed, our genitals and breasts bumping each other. She began to push at me more violently, and then I yielded until she had pushed me first onto my side, and then onto my back. Like a great lizard crawling out of the water onto dry land, she reared herself up, separating her upper body from mine. Her breasts, covered with gleaming sweat, hung down fully, the nipples challenging my eyes. Her belly was relaxed and full and her mouth hung open like a wound. Then, with a long glide, she pressed her cunt into my crotch. I felt my head go back and my knees rise up off the bed. For an instant I felt like a woman, lying back, legs apart, head rolling, while a man hung over me, pushing his cock into my cunt. It was an exciting fantasy and I rode it for as long as it lasted, letting myself be open, letting my body be totally accepting. Her shoulders rounded, and again and again she brought her marvellous pussy down and wrapped it around my screaming cock, bathing me in juices and heat.

Soon her rhythm changed and I found myself moving in unison with her, bringing my ass up off the sheets and fucking her from underneath. She began to go crazy. Her mouth dripped saliva, and strange-sounding words dropped from her lips; her breasts jiggled like a seismograph needle, and her cunt did a dance that is impossible to describe.

I reached up with my hands and began rubbing her all over, putting my fingers in her mouth and grabbing her tits. She started to cry out loud, 'No, no no,' and I reached down and pulled her ass toward me. The cheeks fit perfectly into my palms and I let them ride together, the bouncing cheeks slapping against my palms and fingers. She began to move faster and faster and my fingers beat a drumroll on her ass. She was very close to coming but still holding on inside herself. Then she screamed out, 'Oh, hit me, hit me!' And with that I let all my inhibition loose and, yelling like a savage, began slapping and hitting her ass as hard as I could, spanking and spanking until her entire body started to shake wildly, and with a final cry she convulsed and sank her cunt all the way down on my cock and came with long deep shudders and great flow, raking my chest with her fingernails.

She sat there for a long moment and then sank down onto me. I held her very tightly and she shook with relief and fright. 'Oh, I never . . . never . . . like that,' she mumbled. I continued to hold her, and after a while she calmed down.

We lay that way, half-dozing, half-drifting, for almost an hour, and then I rolled over on my side, bringing her with me. She looked at me with surprise and tenderness. My limp cock was still lodged inside her and began to stir. When she had come, I had held her mind in mine, so that no thoughts could disturb her climax. But now the undischarged sperm in my tubes was clamouring for release. 'Again?' she said. 'I don't think I can do it again.'

'You won't have to do anything,' I said, and slowly began to move inside her. At once her cunt warmed up, not with fires of passion, but with the glow of acceptance. I knew it wouldn't be long and I really didn't want to start on another mutual trip. She lay back relaxed and spread her legs apart. She intuited what was happening and was graciously allowing it. I just wanted her box as a passive receptor, letting itself be entered and fucked. Her cunt opened to me like a mouth. Her ass firmed up and she pushed her pussy up so that I could move in and out of it more easily. Within a minute I felt the call, and with a long inner sigh of happiness, I let the load of sperm well up and come spurting out, and waves of unspotted pleasure rolled through my cock and balls and fingers while she sucked at my tool with her rippling lips.

We both slept for a while, and then, when we got up, there was nothing to say. It wasn't that we were blocked, but that we had both become quite private. I didn't want to spend the night there, and she didn't want to come to my place, so we had a cup of coffee together, and I left.

Walking home, I felt free and easy. At that moment Regina was a dead issue in my heart. The world was filled with intelligent sensitive women,

women who enjoyed fucking and who wouldn't involve me in any nonsense concerning promises. But after getting back, showering, and falling comfortably asleep, nightmares visited me and my dreams were filled with terror. A dozen times figures climbed in through windows to slit my throat and suffocate me with my pillow. Several times I awoke gasping for air, a cold sweat on my forehead.

The next morning I woke up depressed. I was so deeply into the mood that I couldn't just dig it and wait for it to pass. I needed some object to serve as a psychic lighting rod, and the first thing that appeared was an image of Regina in my mind.

Suddenly I was certain that she had betrayed me the night before. It is a curious facet of schizophrenia that, while one portion of the mind understands a reality in a certain way, another portion of the mind can totally negate that perception. And the conflict is so terrible between them that one learns to accept whichever is stronger at the moment, no matter how far out of tune it is.

So Regina became the target, and I bombarded her with missiles of hatred and resentment, launching them three thousand miles to haunt her in California. I mentally destroyed her and then set her astral body in flames. I saw her lying on her bed, her mouth stuffed with cock, her cunt a quivering gift for hundreds of men who passed by daily just to fuck her. And as I ate breakfast, I realised that whatever demons lived in this particular part of my psyche had the upper hand, and there was nothing I could do about it.

(3)

JEALOUSY IS THE most obscene of all human feelings, for it attempts to make human beings into private property; it is an imperialism of the emotions. I lay in bed at night and think of all the women I have ever fucked. I picture their cunts in a giant mosaic on the wall in my mind, and hundreds upon hundreds of the hairy pink slits pile up in a writhing montage of movement and secretion. I don't know how many thousands of times and into how many women I have plunged my cock, so that I am long past the point where there can be any specialness for me in the sensations of any one woman, any one vagina. Each woman is unique, and when I am with her, I am totally with *her*. But all women are the same, so which of the many *hers* it is doesn't particularly matter.

There was a time when I felt cunt to be holy, and to enter a woman was the most sublime and tender of moments. There was a definite religious awe about penetrating past the opening and into the actual body of another human being, especially when that opening led to the deep mysterious folds of birth and consciousness. But in so few instances was my feeling reciprocated, so often did it get lost in the woman's fears and fantasies, that fucking was relegated to an act of mere symbolic sensation. And after a while my sensibilities got dull, and one day I found I was past the point of feeling anything except my own reactions, and knew that I had lost the ability to know the sexual act as something precious.

Yet with that came a new freedom. I learned that what is important is the quality of the act and not the personality of the partner. That is, between two people there can be a bond of tenderness, a great subtlety of communication, a richness of trust. But it is the presence and expression of these qualities from which beauty arises, and it doesn't matter who the people are, at all. I know deep in my heart, that I can have a full and totally satisfying and elevating sexual encounter with a total stranger as well as with a woman I have known for ten years. It's a question of energy flow, and following the logic of that, there can be no room the jealousy, for how long can I deny to any woman what I allow myself?

And yet I do. I have been away from Regina for as long as six months, during that time having intense love affairs, or going to the baths and making it with dozens of men in a single night. And in my egoism, I would tell her about these things. She is not jealous of my physical escapades, but of my emotional attachments. I, on the contrary, bless all her close ties of the heart, but stand guard over her body.

I even told her about Marianne, my Aries poet of the three-week affair. We had met at a party, one of those pseudo-orgies uptown, where everyone is aggressively liberated but shows it by standing around shouting insanities and cackling at full volume. I had had enough hash in me not to care any more, so I took my clothes off and began dancing. Soon I was joined by three others and we spent the night titillating and scandalising the assembled copywriters, account executives and psychiatrists who made up the weird melange. Marianne moved in fast, and before I knew it I had been cut out of the herd, like a cow being manipulated by a smart horse. There were several other chicks in the room who were giving me more interesting signals, but she came on so strong that I let myself get carried away by her.

As might be expected, she had a kid, and was just breaking off a ten-year marriage; had just finished two years of therapy and felt herself completely healthy; and in general possessed all the proper attributes of the neurotic young lady of our time. She had to leave early, and I found myself caught up in the vortex of her energy. 'I'll take you home,' I said. And so we rode all the way downtown in a cab, during which time she reached into my coveralls and played with my cock in such a tantalising fashion as to have me groaning all over the back seat. She was devilish, running her hand down to the base and then skipping up the shaft with her palm and ending by twirling the tips of her fingers around the head. It was the kind of hand job that leaves you tingling at the edge of your come and crying inside for her to put her mouth over the tool and bathe it with warmth and wet, sucking it gently, licking at it with child's tongue, until the geyser roars up and fills her mouth with a throatful of bittersweet sperm.

We got to her place and dropped the kid in bed, and then tore straight for her room. Clothes flew off, and for the next hour it was all sparks. She came at me like a starved dog at a piece of meat. I bucked back at her but she was overwhelming. There was nothing to do but let the Aries power exert itself, and as always in these cases, the wise Scorpio retreated into himself and weathered the blast, knowing that even the strongest of foes one day tires and then lies down. At which time the Scorpion rattles forth and destroys him with a single sting of pure radiant energy.

It was as though she didn't think we would survive until tomorrow and she wanted to squeeze in all sexual experience tonight. She sucked me and forced my mouth to her cunt and spread the lips apart with her fingers so my tongue could penetrate deeper into the twat. She tore at me with her nails and cried in glee when I turned her over and spanked her fat ass. Then I sent her for some vaseline, and had her lubricate her asshole. I took her on her back, throwing back her legs so that her ankles were at her ears, and plunged into the tight waiting hole. She said she had only done this once before and it hadn't gone well, but now she was all ass, quivering, sucking me into her, and letting out groans that rose from her bowels, that hung halfway between pain and pleasure. I pulled out and plunged into her cunt, and we rode for a very long time, neither of us even thinking of coming, since the heat flashes and head trips and the delicious texture of flesh in our hands was so good that we didn't want it to end.

Meanwhile Regina was living the life of a semi-recluse, struggling along on a small welfare cheque, taking care of a four-year-old kid twenty-four hours a day, going to school, teaching dance classes, and keeping a house in order. For weeks she went through the daily grind, each night collapsing into an exhausted sleep. I received letters from her telling me that her life was hard these days, and I wrote back short notes indicating what a wild good time I was having. Finally, after a month of this, she visited with some friends and met a boy of seventeen who had been her neighbour some time back. He was one of those California model youth who smokes a lot of dope, smiles most of the time, says very little, and seems always to have a guitar in the immediate vicinity. She was tired and lonely and horny, and he was passively agreeable to anything. So they rapped, and he took her to a teenage discotheque, where she had a chance to get into what it was to be a teenager again, and had a delightful time. Then he took her home and of course they rapped a bit more and turned on, and soon they were fucking. They fucked two or three times over the next few weeks and then they stopped, because there was nothing else to sustain the relationship, he being so young and all.

In any court of law, of course, Regina would be acquitted. It would be absurd to call what she did infidelity, especially in light of my behaviour. Yet, when I asked her about what she had been doing sexually, and she told me about the adventure, I flew into a towering rage. I called her names. I demanded to know details. It was a dark stormy night, and four times I slammed out of the house into the rain, returning dripping wet, only to begin another round. Luckily I had enough perspective to see the absurdity of the scene, and told her that she should take none of this seriously, because I was simply acting out a fantasy near and dear to me. The actual dynamic was that I could feel the jealousy as long as Regina's body was nearby and accessible, and not have the jealousy overwhelm my basically warm feelings toward her. But now that she was back in California, the recall of the same scene brought up a cold rage, and in my heart I killed her again and again for the foul deed of letting another man fuck her.

She, of course, has her own game, for she never tells me about her sexual affairs right out. The stories always either slip out, or she formulates them in this way, 'Oh, there was another man I forgot to tell you about,' and does that two or three times for each absence we have from one another. In part I think I am being extremely childish, but in another sense I am putting myself through a very special kind of school. Because all of this is pain. Although I am not being fair, although my feelings clash with my intellect, and my body is a blind referee, there is a definite path to my behaviour, a general sense of learning very important lessons about life. I don't know why I should have the university metaphor concerning living or for what cosmic report card I am trying to get good grades, but that is where it is at.

One night, for example, just two weeks after Regina's departure, I spent the evening with a woman I had been eyeing for some time. Ironically, she is in a relationship with a man that perfectly parallels mine with Regina. Only she is playing me to Harry, while Harry is playing Regina to her. Harry, like most men, wants to have his cake and eat it too. He wants Isabel to sit at home and be purringly ready for his pleasure whenever he wants her, and yet to be able to go and come as he pleases, and fuck whom and when he pleases. She, like most women, has no objection to his tomcatting, provided he makes a basic commitment to hearth, home and baby. 'If he would just give me the feeling that I was his woman, then it would be much easier for me to overlook his fucking other chicks,' she said.

I was with her at a time when their relationship was going through one of its endless redefinitions. We smoked some dope and listened to music and talked about only those things which would keep the evening flowing at its fullest and richest. This night I was playing a twentieth-century version of The Purple Mask, 'Secret Agent from the Void Patrol'. I took her precipice-hanging, seeing how close we could get to insanity and social disaster and still maintain perfect control of the situation. Of course, it was a turn-on. It is the city boy's version of taking a chick on a motorcycle. She sits spread-legged on the back, holding on to you for total support, and you open it up very slowly, letting her get used to it, doing fifty, then seventy, then ninety, until you're wide open a hundred and fifteen down the highway and suddenly she realises how fast she's going and it's too late to be scared but still she's terrified and she's holding on so tight she doesn't even realise that her legs are locked and all sensation has been reduced to a great burning in her belly. And when you stop and she gets off, her thighs are trembling and her cunt is wet and her breasts are tender, and it doesn't take anything just to lay her down on the grass and pull her jeans off, and fuck her like she's never known she could have it before.

But then the phone rang. It was Harry. He was tripping and down. He had spent the entire day having a fine old time with some friends, but now the energy was running down and he was feeling like a lost little boy, and he wanted Isabel to comfort him. But Isabel was now out on a trip through the cosmos with me, and didn't really want to get all involved in personality games at the level he suggested. Yet she couldn't hang up. So this incredibly long tedious conversation went on, in which she kept telling him over and over again that she had said everything she wanted to say, and had heard everything she wanted to hear, and then would get sucked into another round of his trip, and it would be followed by a long series of 'Yes, buts'. I got disgusted after five minutes and went to take a shower. I wondered whether he could hear the water running, and how that made him feel. Probably the way I would feel in such a circumstance. Then I thought, 'The way I *have felt* in such circumstances.' Anger rose up in me. 'Fuck,' I said to myself, 'I've paid my dues in this area. If he is still shmucking around out there in the sexual boondocks, that is no skin off my ass. I can have compassion, but I can't save his soul for him.' I thought of the theatre of cruelty, and it occurred to me that he too was learning, learning from his pain, learning from my indifference and from the coolness of his chick.

I dressed and went out. The Christian part of my personality made one last attempt. I said to her, 'Should I leave? If he wants to come over . . .' But she shook her head and waved her hand for me to sit next to her. I sat down and she put her hand right on my thigh and began stroking up and down the length of it. Like a good old Pontius Pilate, I washed my hands of the matter.

Then an odd thing happened. I suddenly realised that there were three of us in the room. The fact that Harry was on the telephone and not literally physically present made no real difference. His consciousness was as immediate as hers and mine. But he couldn't see what was happening! I reached over and kissed her throat very gently. I could hear, from a distance, Harry's insistent voice over the phone. I began nibbling at her neck and moved up to her ear, where I started to breathe and tongue and kiss the lobes and shell, and right into the centre of the opening. It was strange, because in one ear she was getting the verbal communication from Harry through the phone, and in the other ear she was receiving my tactile messages. It was impossible to tell how she was reacting to each element. It was all a mix.

Inwardly, I hoped Harry would have the breadth and humour to appreciate this if he ever found out. And I said a prayer for myself, that when I found myself in his shoes, especially with Regina, I too could maintain the necessary perspective.

I moved my hands down and started to massage her neck. I didn't know what the limits on the game were, so I decided to see how far it all went. I reached under her blouse and cupped a full breast in my hand. She slumped forward and then jerked back and said into the receiver, 'No, no, I'm still here, I'm just listening'. Incredible! He had picked up on her shift in attention over the phone. I leaned forward and sucked one pink nipple into my mouth, licking under it to take the full weight of her breast on my tongue. She began to writhe and pushed me away. I looked up at her and her eyes told me that she couldn't keep the phone conversation going if I really began to touch her.

I got up to walk around and came back again, only to start another round of the game. This time I moved my hands over her thighs and belly, and then pulled one leg to the side so that she sat with her knees out, her cunt a provocative bulge through the pants. I stroked the outline of the lips through the cloth and slid my other hand under her so that her ass rested on it.

Harry said something and she laughed. The sound startled me, and I looked over to her. I couldn't tell what she was responding to, and then realised it didn't matter. Throwing all caution to the sky I brought my hand up hard around her cunt and covered her breast with my mouth again. This time she went slack and I felt all over her body, stroking and kneading, kissing and holding, while she listened and talked into the receiver. The scene became very Fellini and finally she hung up.

'He may come over,' she said to me.

Now there was a problem, for if we fucked, there was the chance he would walk in at any moment. And how could we enjoy it fully with our ears attuned for any slight sound on the stairs? The best way to deal with any problem is to sail into the face of it, ready to alter course on the spot, but not making any major navigational changes because of fear.

I drew her to me and we lay down on the couch, fully dressed, in one another's arms. It was like teenager days, and a flash of Regina and her young man went through my mind. At that moment, with Isabel breathing on my face, pressing her delicious young body against me, there was no jealousy toward Regina for anything she had done. It amazed me that so long as I felt I was being wanted and loved, I had no fear about anything Regina did. Was jealousy then a fear of loss, a sense of being left out?

We kissed, and it was one of those long, involved kisses like a dance. We lay in perfect attention, fully aware of what our lips and tongues were doing, aware of the taste of saliva and the promise of opening. I bit at her gently, and she took my tongue between her teeth and squeezed it. Yet, for all the concentration at our mouths, we remained aware of the rest of the room, and of the fact that Harry might walk in an any minute. We were abyss-slumming again, litterbugging in the void.

We seemed to have matched rhythms perfectly for the evening, probably because both of us were completely up for pleasing one another. After the long kiss, we pulled back and spent another long time looking into each other's eyes. It was that exquisite time when inner consciousness and outer reality are felt as one and the same thing.

There was no difference between me and her, merely distinctions. Her thoughts flowed as mine did, but we were unconcerned with content, only with structure. Our heads merged and we merged with everything around us, and slowly our bodies found their own movement, an easy pumping ride of the pelvis rocking into pelvis.

Never had the moment been so right for fucking. The thought hit both of us simultaneously, and as one, our minds reached for the space outside the door where Harry might burst in at any moment. Ambivalence reached the level of pain. And then in a blinding flash of insight, I had the solution. It was, to be sure, a cop-out, since true bravery – or stupidity – would have involved taking the scene to whatever conclusion *it* dictated. But since turning thirty I am sometimes content with a symbolic victory over circumstances, bringing matters to a rational conclusion 'A blow job would meet the situation perfectly,' I said.

She looked at me for a long time, and then a smile began playing at the corner of her mouth. 'We would both be dressed,' I continued. 'And if Harry didn't come, we could go right on with it, and if he did, we could pull it together fast enough so it would seem that we were just sitting together on the couch.' It was preposterous, of course. As jealous as he would be at the moment if he came in, he would know immediately what had been going on. But it was a clever enough rationalisation to allow us to do what we wanted to do anyway.

I closed my eyes and felt her hands begin to roam over my chest. She was really good. Her tongue found my face and them moved to my ear. She came close to driving me mad with lust, working delicately and consciously, varying her breath and the movement of her lips, tantalising, drawing me out, and then plunging her tongue home. I cried out and felt my pelvis moving involuntarily. She whispered to me, 'Everything we do from now on is a prelude to me sucking you off.' This was her way of telling me to let go and relax, that she was in control. I gladly relinquished all power into her hands.

She moved down, tonguing my nipples and

belly, and then taking a long time to rim my belly button, working into it hard. I pushed my belly out into her face, opening the symbolic cunt to her mouth. She bit into the soft flesh and brought a mouthful of skin into her mouth, nibbling and tearing, licking, sucking. I grabbed her hair and forced her face deeper into my soft centre. She moaned and began to move her head up and down, covering the entire area with long flat strokes of her tongue, lapping like a deer at a salt lick. The movement got larger and soon she was licking into my pubic hair and over my thighs, running her now dry rasping tongue into the space between thighs and balls, the sensitive joint which is hardly ever touched. I brought my legs together and clamped her head between them. She hung there for a moment, pinned, and then dropped down, nuzzling between my legs and licking at the underpart of my balls.

Already I felt myself coming, and I wanted to hold it back, to enjoy just the feeling of her working her mouth over me. Suddenly there was a creak outside the door and both of us sat bolt upright in sheer terror. A long instant passed and then we heard footsteps moving past. We looked at each other and giggled in relief. But the sexual thread was threatening to snap. I reached for her and roughly brought her chest to my mouth. I pulled up her shirt again and took her sharply-sloped tit into me. She buckled at once, and as I sucked hard at her nipple, feeling the velvety texture making love to my tongue, she reached down and grabbed my cock, this time pulling at it in long deep movements. I let her breast go and leaned back again, and now she went at it with a will. We knew that we couldn't survive another shock like the one which had just happened. So she opened her mouth wide and brought it right over my now throbbing cock. With one hand at the base, pulling, jerking it off, she covered the shaft with loose lips and hot tongue, making slurping sounds all over me.

I began to move. Without any control, my ass jerked up and forward, and I rode my cock into her luscious mouth, feeling the rising heat and pleasure. She sucked hard, with a will to bringing me off. She curled her body up and bunched herself over my legs. It was as though she were drawing herself up into the foetal position. She made small whimpering sounds, almost like a baby, and I felt the splash of tears on my belly. She seemed to be squeezing something out of herself and the focus for her act was drawing the sperm out of my cock. For an instant I flashed our mutual aloneness, each of us working out some inner drama and using the other as a tool to bring it off. But it didn't matter, for already I could feel the scalding sperm bubbling in my balls; I could feel the waves of release coming from as far away as my toes and fingers. I was breathing deeply and fully, and my body worked like a bellows, gathering all the energy into a mighty ball in my bowels. And then, as I began to buck and shout, and she moaned into my cock, frantically working her tongue and sucking so hard that her cheeks caved in, I let the sperm come spurting out, jet after jet, and like somebody who has been on the desert for a day and has just been presented with a juicy orange, she sucked and lapped and ate until there was absolutely nothing left, and then collapsed, her cheek on my thigh, my now limp cock still in her mouth.

We lay together for a long while, and then she got up. I pulled my pants up and we sat and drank some juice. Small talk followed, and sleepiness. I felt very tender and fond towards Isabel, and, if truth must be told, just a little bit in love with her already. She was cold, so we took a blanket and I covered us with it while she snuggled into my arms. For a long time we just felt one another's presence, the breathing, the basic body warmth. And then she stirred. 'I wonder if I should call Harry back?' she said.

And I laughed. For how many times in the past, after making it with someone, did I feel a real desire to be with my mate of the time? It was as though one purged oneself of the desire to assert one's independence, one asserted one's liberty, and then, having done so, wanted to make it back to the current partner. For an instant I thought how nice it would be if Regina were here and then I could go romp with Isabel while she did a thing with Harry. Maybe in the open exchange of partners, there might be a solution to the problem of freedom in mating. But then, if the foursome got tight enough, the people in it would want to be asserting their freedom from the group, and begin making it with yet others. My mind quickly raced to the logical extension and I thought, 'What if everybody in the world were fucking everybody else, and we had no stupid distinctions as to "mine" and "yours", would the species then be totally one, or would it find yet more diabolical forms of infidelity?' The problem, as always, returned to the basic question: 'Is the human race basically fucked?' If so, then nothing we do can do anything but add to confusion and misery. In which case the only proper approach is laughter.

And so I continued to laugh. And Isabel was quite puzzled by my reaction. 'By all means, call him,' I said. 'I think it's a perfect gesture.' But there was no malice in my cynicism, and for a fleeting moment I wished Regina were there to share the humour of the situation with me, for above all, she has a mind sharp enough to see the ludicrous.

In a while I left, with Isabel vainly making phone calls trying to track Harry down. Since I am involved with both of them in several business and personal enterprises, I knew I would be seeing them again, together and separately. I wondered whether she would tell him, and what his response would be. Life was very interesting the minute one understood it as theatre, and one's overriding value became one of style and integrity.

I slept badly, and in the morning, before breakfast, there was a letter from Regina waiting for me, the first one since her return to the Coast.

(4)

THE MINUTE I saw her handwriting, my heart melted. In the middle of the most tortuous changes and seeming resolutions not to have anything to do with her again, a simple sheet of paper from California reduced me to jelly. I had been walking down the street a few days earlier, thinking of nothing in particular, when I suddenly saw Regina's naked body in bed. She was lying on her side, and moving into a man's arms. I could see her ass tighten as she brought her thighs up to his, and then her arms moved round his shoulders in order to bring his face to her lips. I froze on the spot, standing stock still on the sidewalk. A spasm of jealousy seized me like a foot cramp and I felt my face screw up in rage while my hands began to shake. Luckily, I was on Avenue A and 4th Street, where such behaviour doesn't seem odd to anyone.

I probed deeper to find out who she was with, and then realised that the man of the fantasy had to be a man that I put there. And I wondered why I was picturing her with someone else and not myself. Was I on a secret unworthiness trip, or working out yet another kink of the bi-sexual scene; or was it that I was afraid to let myself know how much I wanted to be with her? So long as I was jealous, I couldn't feel longing or loss or love. So I put up the screen of suspicion to keep me from coming to terms with my actual feelings. And the minute I felt that, pang after pang of desolation shot through me, and I found myself calling out 'Regina' on the street.

The letter had some chitchat about the state of the garden and the bell-clear days that were now visiting Mendocino, and lines speaking about her love for me and faith in my actually getting a relationship with her that had some permanence. I swung from elation to depression. Again I felt that hand of responsibility creeping toward my throat, the feeling that there was something I 'ought' to be doing or feeling. I realised that this was at least half in my head, and that there were millions of people the world over who lived in complete solitude and lovelessness; and here I was complaining because this woman wanted to make a life with me.

I looked around my apartment. Theoretically, I had everything I wanted. A big enough place of my own in the East Village, enough money to live on without having to work for a year, friends and women all close to hand, and the chance to work at what I am good at and receive pay and recognition for what I do. And yet it was empty. Only in those manic moments when I was 'on' did the whole scene mean anything. Somehow, without a woman who was special, without a mate, I was incomplete, and no amount of social gloss could fill the gap. This much was clear; the question then became, was Regina that woman? And how does one go about making such a judgement? How could I think in terms of measurement?

My mind sped back to the scenes we'd been in, and all the bummers lined up in one ledger while all the good trips lined up in another. I couldn't begin to give them values in order to weigh them. I remembered the time I met her. It was at a big registration day meeting at the Berkeley Free University. I was teaching a workshop in relaxation and breathing, and she was doing a dance number. I had heard her name as someone to see, and I found where she was sitting. At first I was disappointed. I had expected a very young, blonde chick with slow knowing eyes; Regina was clearly close to thirty, and very nervous, with eyes that came across like a self-conscious cash register. She was married at the time, and she introduced me to her old man. I saw at once that they weren't making it, a flash that was substantiated later. I went about to do some things and then somebody threw a long piece of rock on the stereo and I began dancing. I saw Regina across the way and beckoned to her. We danced toward each other, and for about twenty minutes worked everything out with our bodies. It got to be pure fucking, although most people don't know how to look at dance so they missed the scene, except for the Communications Company, who came up after the record ended and gave me a pornographic magazine, with comic-book drawings of Antony and Cleopatra.

I got to rapping to her old man and dug they were at a place where they could use a third to catalyse their mix. I knew it was tricky but as Jud once put it, 'Threesomes are chic.' I made a mental note to visit them one night soon and see if we could get it off and get it on.

But before that happened, two days later she called me. 'Come over,' she said. And in her voice was a fucking summons, clear as a bell. I didn't like being thrown off balance in this way, because I operate best when I move at my own rhythm. But I went, and as I suspected, her old man wasn't home. She was pretty frantic and hopping all around the place and what I wanted to do most was to get her to sit down and relax before anything else happened. But she had a programme in her head and marched us both through it in double-time. She put on a record, danced for three minutes, put her arms around my neck, and dragged me down to the mattress. I knew it was wrong as it happened, wrong timing, wrong vibrations. Then the bombshell. 'I've never come with a man,' she said. 'I know you can make me come.'

Of course, the thing to have done was to rise up immediately and state, 'I can't make anybody do anything,' and split. But the old ego was at work, getting all puffed up. I had a small reputation around the school as a man who knew and understood what women's bodies needed. And here I was being consulted on a special case!

Off with our clothes! And before I knew it, I had an erection, was inside her, and came, all before I had a chance to catch my breath. Inside she was moving so fast that she literally speeded time up, and I felt like a man who steps into an elevator shaft expecting to find an elevator there but getting a nasty surprise. I lay on her in full shock, my cock shrinking quickly and my ego hightailing it out of sight. Regina's face was as hard as stone and her eyes told me how much she despised me at the moment. I had been suckered into committing the crime, then was caught, tried, convicted and executed, all within half an hour. Somewhere inside me I took my hat off to the lady. Any woman who can cut my balls off without my even noticing until it was too late, deserves accolades. At last, I had found a bitch to match the bastard in me.

Ah, but what a naive, inexperienced, self-conscious bitch she was. Nothing of the pirate about her; she did all her work in the make-believe dark of her supposed unconscious mind. I rolled off and lit a cigarette. For the first time I was able to look at her body. She was really exquisite, with an ass made to be worshipped, it was so full, so dense, so invitingly tough, made to be fucked and licked and spanked. Any woman with an ass like that couldn't be all bad, reasoned my atavistic mind.

We rapped about nothing at all, just to fill the space until my cock got hard again and we could fuck once more. Clearly, the guru was getting a second chance. I bided my time and let the juices fill up and recharge in my balls, and only when I knew I was ready for another assault did I reach over and cup her breast. A long shudder ran through her.

She was on a heavy breast trip, and had nursed her kid for almost three years. She still had some milk left and as I went down on the luscious nipple, the warm fluid spurted into my mouth. She was moaning and kicking her legs and I put my hand down to her thighs and found that her cunt was really wet this time. Not so bad, I thought to myself, it's just a matter of finding the right buttons to push. But then, a cry from the next room. It was her kid. Shit! What a time. I had heard that kids are jealous buggers and don't miss a chance to fuck up the action when they can.

But she put her hands on the back of my head and pushed my mouth onto her tit again. She was really hot and not about to be interrupted.

I dove into the fleshy warm jiggling breast again, and glued my lips to her wrinkled tit. Only this time it was a different kid of sucking. I wanted milk. It was sexy but in an entirely different way. I brought the entire breast into my mouth and pulled on it for all I was worth, and to my squirming delight, mouthful after mouthful of milk spilled onto my tongue.

Far out! But I had a more complex trip going, because I could feel my cock beginning to sound its ancient call. 'Cunt,' it cried. 'Give me cunt.'

With that I mounted her like a cavalry man climbing aboard his steed. She looked at me with shock and surprise and admiration. With a blow I had slain the Freudian dragon, and her now hot cunt opened and welcomed me in with a great hurrah. I began to move slowly, feeling the sublime squishiness of her pussy sliding under me. It seemed like a box made of quicksand, rolling from side to side, bubbling up from the deep centre and enveloping my cock, and then giving way to let me sink deep into her. She made almost no sound, but her mouth opened in a silent cry. It was as though her entire body went into a single prolonged spasm, and she held onto it, using it as a centre around which she moved her legs and arms. Her head rolled from side to side, and her eyes closed. I looked down as though from a great height. 'Regina!' I called, but she didn't seem to hear me.

The kid was sleeping, Regina was tripping on some intense inner sexual drama, and I was left dutifully moving my cock in and out of her, feeling the sensations, but somehow not connected with anything. I thought it would be as good a time as any to see what I could find out about the mechanics of her cunt, and perhaps do something about making her come.

I moved back and dropped my pelvis so I could bring my cock in from a lower angle. Immediately I felt the difference in heat and penetration. I flashed the connection and brought my cock to bear inside her. But no sooner had I found a beautiful inner niche to lodge the head of my prick, she bucked back and froze. Her eyes opened and I got the hate glance again. 'It hurts there!' she said, almost spitting at me. 'Excuse me,' I said, 'no harm intended.' She stuck out her chin and turned her head to the side as though waiting for a blow, but I bowed out, and in a moment she relaxed and lay back down. I began moving again, slowly, and again she caught the rhythm of my rod and started to groove on it. Again I felt as though I was on the outside looking in and this time reached under her legs to bring them back to her chest. I raised them half a foot when she went rigid again. 'I don't want to put my legs that way,' she said.

I got pissed. 'Well, what the fuck do you want?' I screamed. 'It hurts this way, you don't want to do it that way. Why don't you just go fuck yourself?!' To my surprise, she burst into tears. 'That's what I usually have to do,' she said. 'All men are so insensitive and don't know how to touch me and then they blame me for being frigid. I wind up having to masturbate.'

Now, it's a funny thing about sophistication. If anybody else had made that speech under any other circumstances, I would have properly sneered and made some inner gesture concerning the sorrow of sexual unhappiness in the world, and then quoting Dylan to the effect that 'it's not my problem', split. But she had the Indian sign on me, and before I could catch myself, I had fallen into a pseudo women's lib conversation concerning the plight of the female in male chauvinist America. Of course I understood. Of course I was not like all those other nasty men. Of course she could give herself totally to me, if I would just have patience. Wasn't she a prize worth waiting for, worth cultivating? And when she was all mine, no other man would have what I have.

Like an idiot, I fell for it. Partially, I suppose, because it was true. But truth merely indicates, it does not prescribe. Something in me needed to run this particular treadmill. We talked for a few minutes, and then she asked if I would get off her, because I was getting heavy. That snapped it. I reared back and laid my hands on her shoulders and then leaned forward, pinning her with my full weight. She tried to struggle but I had her at three points, and now brought my cock into equal pressure with my hands. 'I don't feel like fucking anymore,' she said. 'That's too bad,' I told her.

And of course, she yielded, as a woman always does when a stiff cock starts churning inside her cunt. They may protest the circumstances, or the person, but if a man really has it hard and is really tuned in to what is happening, he can fuck any woman for hours. Put it in her and she'll moo with contentment. And so it happened. But I wasn't counting on the physiological trap, and this time there was no creamy secretion, only a thin spiteful dribble. And there was no heat, only a clammy blandness of temperature. And nothing I did helped. I sucked her breasts again and tried kissing her, and grabbed her ass to bring her cunt close up to my crotch. And she went with it all, seemingly digging it all, but not yielding any of her juices. It was impossible to tell whether she was holding back with her mind, or whether the flow was beyond her control and wouldn't come whether she wanted it or not. I was past figuring it out and past caring, and just slid my cock in and out of her, concentrating on my own sensations, using her like a hand to jerk off in, falling into the most sluttish fantasies to compensate for the thin reality. 'She's just a pig,' went the refrain in my mind. 'Anyone can have her. She's a frigid bitchy middle-aged-middle-class whore who doesn't have enough sense to know what she is. She probably fucks for anyone who'll open his zipper. She's probably gone down on half the school, sucking off students ten years younger than she is in telephone booths at the back of the cafeteria. How many men has she dragged up here with the same plea: "make me come"?' And as the fantasy convoluted, I became excited. I looked down at her, at the woman's body lying underneath me.

Without planning it, I pulled out of her fast. She opened her eyes in surprise and dismay. I grabbed her thighs and pushed her to the side. She got the idea and rolled over. She lay on her belly, her ass forming a gorgeous mound for my eyes, her thick dancer's thighs looking very vulnerable, and between them the cunt hair peeking out. I pulled her ass up to bring her to her knees. And then leaned forward to shove her shoulders down, so that her ass stuck up and exposed the pink slit of her pussy more fully. I knelt between her legs and pried the cheeks apart. Her clenched asshole warned me away from it, and the tension in her body almost made me forget the entire thing. But this was the last one, I thought. I'd never be making it again with this bitch, so I might as well get off as good a fuck as I could.

I leaned forward and felt that delicious moment when the head of my cock slides past the feathery touch of the outer cunt lips, meets the massaging pressure of the inner lips, and then sloshes happily and warmly into the very cunt centre, that wrinkled bud that is so tightly closed and stretches so tautly to embrace the entire shaft of the cock, from the sensitive head to the broad thick base. I heard her sigh. I moved in very slowly, angling up slightly and aiming right at the cervix. But I was only three-quarters in when she tightened up. 'You're hurting me again,' she hissed. For an instant I wanted to just slap her until she, once and for all, stopped the whining, the inability to withstand just a little pain in order to find a greater pleasure. It was not the fact that she announced I was hurting her that bothered me, but the way she presented it, as though it were a non-negotiable demand for me to stop fucking her altogether. But either I didn't have the energy or the time wasn't right, and I pulled back. I brought my cock to the point where the tip of it was right at the opening to her cunt. I nudged in and opened her up gently, and then pulled back and watched the pink membrane close up right after me. I poked in again, and then out. She gasped and wiggled her ass. It was a kind of genital foreplay and ordinarily is just the prelude to deeper things, but I knew this was as much as she could take, so we did it that way. It was like getting a blow job where the lips never leave the head, and although

I wanted time and again to shove it all the way up her hole, I contented myself to feeling the heat vibrations dance around the tip of my tool, and then, moving faster, felt the come beginning to stir at the shaft of my cock. I reached down and pried her buttocks apart. I could see the cunt, now wet, sloppily sloshing as it sucked at my prick. I reached lower and opened her cunt with my fingers. She shuddered a bit and grabbed the sheet with her fingers, clenching the fabric into a ball.

The space filled with the heady aroma of cunt goo and now her secretion became the thick white flow that marks real sexual excitement. I flashed the thought that perhaps I could do it, could get her to come. But already I felt the summons deep inside me. I rode, gingerly and tingling, to a small, local, intense orgasm, feeling it all in the head of my cock, coming with most of my tool still outside her, and just the tip spouting the sperm into her blind gash. There was a long dislocated moment, in which I felt myself as myself, and felt her as her, and was aware of some invisible bond which held us together, some kind of relationship that had no name or form or meaning, but just was. Again, I felt us an 'us' although all my conscious faculties would have nothing to do with the idea.

I pulled my cock out and she fell face forward on the bed. I sat down where I was kneeling and looked at her. She rolled over and her face presented me with a delightful surprise, for she was relaxed and smiling and warm. 'Ohh,' she said, 'that was wonderful.' And then slid over and put her head in my lap and her arms around my waist. I suddenly felt good all over and lay down beside her, pulling her into my arms and close to my chest, and suddenly feeling the human warmth that had been missing during the fucking, that quality of person which can't be defined but is necessary if the soul is not to die of thirst.

Two years had passed since that moment, and in essence, nothing had changed. But what we have become with each other is immeasurably deeper and richer, there is a fullness that goes beyond the meagre faculties of consciousness to understand. She is still a bitch and I am still a madman, and yet, no matter how I twist or turn, I find her.

And running in opposition is my total desire for freedom, to have no human being depend on me, to have no one be able to say I must be in a certain place at a certain time. Now that the revolution is exploding, now that I am reaching a fullness of power and insight, there is a sense of propulsion, a sense of wanting to discard all name and costume, and hurl myself out into the nothingness on a long single fiery trajectory into the final end. And yet I walk, step by step, into the arms of the woman who may be nothing but an early deafness and suffocation.

There are a thousand, a hundred thousand I's inside me, countless masks and costumes. All the conditioning of my youth, the training that made

me a priest a communist a bisexual a fascist a poet
a drug addict a teacher a cosmic protoplasmic
blip, and all the racial archetypes of the entire
species, are continually screaming for recognition,
for energy. They all want expression in the social
world, to be formed, to be applauded. And inside,
there are as many voices clamouring for concentration, for solitude, for irony, for disdain.

And so, who am I? There is no answer to this
question. There is only the continual asking and
the dizzying stream of suggested response which
are no more than gestures in the grand pantomime
of Shiva. Here I sit with two dreams beckoning,
and there is no way for me to know what to do
except watch myself as each day passes, and learn
to know where I go and what I do. And one day
I may learn how the whole thing turns out.

I stayed with Regina for the whole evening, and
later went back to my place, where Kathy was
waiting for me. Kathy was more or less living with
me at the time. Her old man, Jimmy, had just
split for Pakistan and she decided to come crash
at my pad. We had fucked a bit, but she was still
hung up over Jimmy, with whom she had been
living for two years. Besides that, she was bisexual
and came on very suspicious of my own bi trip.
She had just been in Sonoma for a few days,
seeing some people. We were very glad to see
each other, and decided to turn on. She laid her

trip on me and I told her about the scene with Regina.

'Far out,' she said. There was a long silence. 'Would you like to meet her?' I asked. She smiled her wicked smile, the space between her two front teeth very suggestive. 'It might be interesting,' she said. 'She's got a nice cunt,' I added, 'if you can get it hot.' She stood up. 'Might be worth a try. I haven't had a woman for a while.'

I got up also. 'Maybe you and I could work out a few things this way too.' The decision made, we threw on our jackets, and went over to visit Regina.

(5)

·LIKE MOST PEOPLE, I had been raised with the myth that we first make decisions consciously and rationally, and then act on them. A great deal of experience went into teaching me that we come to decisions out of a vast complex of motivations and conditionings and influences which range from pre-natal trauma to the position of the stars. The course of action is, as it were, set independently of that thing we laughingly call 'will', and all our rationalisations are simply excuses we give ourselves to make us more comfortable with whatever it is we have to do anyway. With that understanding, I once and for all dropped all efforts to try to understand why I do things the way I do.

On the way over to Regina's I pondered the

situation. Here were three people largely unsettled and confused about life. Each had tried to come to terms with his or her condition in the single most damaging manner: linking up with someone else who was equally fucked up. The matter was compounded and the ensuing situations brought forth the usual tedious round of hostility and lack of communication and recriminations. Now Regina and her old man were about to split up, as had Kathy with hers, as had I with my woman of several months earlier. Why then, I asked myself, was I acting as agent to bring together yet another menage?

There was, of course, a cornucopia of answers. The ones which came most readily to mind were mischief and messianism. Part of me was excited 'just to see what would happen'. Yet another part, having dutifully read *Stranger in a Strange Land*, was on a communal family trip, and almost immediately I had visions of Kathy and Regina and me living in happy orgiastic community, and then adding on other water brothers and water sisters, and me, probably, operating as the man from Mars. I think it took the form of madness I then affected to breed the self-confidence to pull such tricks off.

We went into Regina's and I entered first. She saw me and her face lit up. Then she saw Kathy, and her mouth tightened. 'Hello,' I said, pointing to Kathy, 'this is the other woman in my life. I thought it would be nice if the two of you met.'

This was clearly a ploy to force recognition of the principle that there should be no jealousy, and we could all be open with each other.

The predictable moment of awkwardness lasted but a brief second and then Regina said, 'Would you like to have some coffee?' Kathy looked at her and the two women sized each other up quickly and fully. It was one of the most open untainted glances I had ever seen and for an instant I felt the full power of womanhood when it is not masked behind the social roles of servility and ineptitude that seem to be the woman's mask in our civilisation. Regina spoke. 'I don't mind sharing him,' she said. Kathy smiled at her. 'There's also us,' she said.

Regina had never made it with a woman and this frank confrontation brought a blush of confusion to her cheeks. We hadn't been here three minutes and already the tension skewed the energy fields among us like the Ames perception rooms in psychology labs, where all the usual cues are changed, and size and distance play strange tricks with one another. Kathy moved right in and went for the coffee pot. 'I'll help you make coffee,' she said.

Suddenly I realised I had to leave the room. I was relatively straight with each of them, but they needed to get it on with each other, and I went into the living room to put some music on and remove my presence from their encounter with one another. It was quite comfortable; I found

Casals playing Bach's suite for unaccompanied cello, and I took off my clothes and began dancing in the empty space. The house had a feeling of great calm: Danny, the little boy, asleep in the back, and two women bustling in the kitchen. Despite the supposed sexual irregularity being proposed, it just seemed like a quiet evening at home.

They came in with the coffee, and when they saw me naked, exchanged knowing glances and laughed. For the first time, I began to feel uncomfortable. I had unconsciously assumed that this would be an analogue to a harem scene, and that I would move my wives around at will, but I flashed that they had come very quickly to some sort of deep understanding which left me outside of that particular bond. Feeling not a little foolish, I suspected they were doing a little-boy ploy with me, and I extricated myself from the mood at once.

I sat down for coffee and Regina went for some grass; Kathy began prowling the apartment, like a cat who needs to sniff a new place all over before getting comfortable in it. I was looking for us to coalesce, but I decided not to try to force anything. Regina came back and we rolled joints and smoked a little in silence, and after a while a kind of relaxation settled over us. 'Are we here for the night?' I asked. The women looked at each other and then back at me. 'At least for the night,' said Kathy.

In a flash, I saw their clothes fall off as they sat there, and I realised that in a short time I would probably be having both of them. As it turned out, that was a naive formulation, but for the moment I allowed myself to indulge in all the pretty pictures of what would happen. I would have them kneel at the edge of the bed, asses high, and stand behind them, putting my cock first in one cunt and then the other, switching quickly, to see if I could feel the tactile difference, the inequalities in heat and moisture. And when they embraced, Kathy's slightly pendulous breasts would cover and enfold Regina's smaller tits and they would grow wild as their nipples rubbed together. I had never been with two women who would make it with each other as well as me, and I was congratulating myself on solving the problem of the eternal triangle. There was, it seemed, nothing easier, and I wondered why somebody hadn't thought of it before.

I got up and went into the bedroom, and with great care smoothed out the sheets and covered the whole thing with a white fur rug that was lying on the floor, and then lay down in the centre of it, pasha-like, waiting for the harem to file in. Which, in a few minutes, they did. Kathy looked at me and her upper lip curled. 'Well, you've done it again,' she said.

They came around to either side of the bed and then slowly began taking their clothes off. It was an indelibly beautiful moment. First shirts, revealing the vulnerable throats and biteable shoulders and maddening female breasts. And the pants, sliding slowly down the thighs and past the knees, and finally having to lift one leg to pull the trouser off, and then the other leg, and all the while the V of their crotches shifting and peeking from under their panties. Two of them! I couldn't believe my luck. And now the final article, as they seemed to bend over in unison to slide the flimsy fabric down, their asses out and that look of expectant concentration that comes on a woman's face when she removes the most intimate garment.

Then they came forward and kneeled on the bed, one on either side. I opened my arms and they came forward, each laying her head on one of my shoulders and sliding her body up, each taking one of my legs and wrapping her legs around it. At each hip I felt the hard pubic bone and the bristly hair and the soft cunt lips pressing in.

At first, there was no actual sexual flash. A conscious awkwardness hung over everything. I breathed a silent prayer, saying, 'Lord, if I must go, let it be at a time like this.' And then the tension melted. All the pictures I had in my head dissolved, and the reality of the moment came crashing home. I leaned my head to one side and felt Kathy's knowing and salacious mouth on my own. Even in kissing, she was able to manage mockery, and her tongue teased at me, wanting me to go over the edge of passion, to become vulnerable, so that she would then have the decision as to whether to join me or not. She wanted to remain cool and aloof, getting her pleasure from the control room. Regina ran her hands up and down the other side, her fingers doing a tentative dance over my nipple and down to my belly and then twirling into my pubic hair. She slithered down over the top of my thigh and between my legs, to send a shuddering spurt of tingling delight throughout my body. At that, she smiled and licked her lips, and began the slow descent of my body with her mouth. She went slowly, with great hesitation, and although I liked the quality of tentativeness, I was impatient. I put my hand down and cupped her head. She looked up at me and said, 'I've never sucked a man before.' The announcement stunned me. 'A lot of men have wanted me to, but I never could make myself do it.' She looked at both us us. 'Now, it feels all right.'

She went consciously towards my cock as Kathy and I watched. Her mouth opened slightly, and paused half a inch away from the head. She began breathing out, and my cock tingled from the warm air bathing it. Everything she did was with delicacy and awareness. She leaned down and moved in for what seemed an eternity, until that single tingling moment when her lips just barely grazed the tip of the tool and she kissed it gently and reverently. Then she dropped her head forward and let her mouth descend on the shaft. She kept her jaw and lips relaxed, and the cock slid in slowly, parting her lips as it entered. I felt faint as I watched inch after inch disappear, watching her lips stretch in a beautiful, obscene embrace over the taut skin. And then, from inside, her tongue started a dance over the entire length of my cock. I was torn between the desire to watch more and the need to fall back and let the pleasure ripples wash over me. Regina moved her head back and I saw the cock emerge, now glistening with wetness, and then she came down and sucked it all in again; her tongue lapped softly and warmly, licking the cock lovingly, and cooing sounds came from deep in her throat.

'God, that looks good!' said Kathy, and she moved down to put her mouth alongside Regina's. I leaned back then, and waited for the feeling of having both their mouths covering me. But Regina pulled herself back and I felt my cock grow cool in the air. There was some motion by my thighs, and I looked down to find the two of them with their mouths glued together, their arms around one another's waists, and their legs intertwined like vines around a rod. For a moment I was disgruntled at having my pleasure cut off so abruptly, but immediately new possibilities offered themselves.

I sat up and watched. The sight filled my eyes the way a Boston cream pie fills my mouth. Too much richness to take in all at once. For a moment it looked like a woman lying next to a mirror, with the mirror making subtle changes. Regina's great ass tightened and loosened, moved back and forth as she brought her cunt to bear against Kathy's box. And opposite, Kathy's smaller ass, which was flabbier but more knowing, looser but more decadent, rode in a small jiggling rhythm as she used her cunt more expertly, dipping the pubic bone down and thrusting it between Regina's thighs. Their mouths were as engulfing as elephant cunts, and they sucked and bit at each others lips and tongues, as though it were a matter of life and death to draw some vital fluid out of the other's body.

At this point it was pure flaming passion, with no self-consciousness or effort. The fire seared them both and they were groping now with their hands, taking their fill of one another's asses and backs and faces. Regina made a sound like buttons running down the ribs of a washboard when a shirt is being scrubbed, and then collapsed suddenly, letting her body go small and burying her face in Kathy's throat. Her knees buckled and she drew them towards her belly. Kathy propped herself up on one elbow and with her other hand reached down slowly, deliberately, and cupped Regina's cunt. For a long while Regina just lay there, and then her legs began to open, majestically. Kathy's hand went lower and I watched her put a single finger forward, up, and just barely between Regina's cunt lips. She sighed a long quavering sigh, and her head came back, and her face came up. She had the look of a saint with a beatific vision. She opened her eyes and found herself staring full into Kathy's face. Within a split second a universe of changes took place in her, all her conditioning and emotions and ideas about things rushed past with lightning speed, were checked and discarded, and what was left was the sense of pure bliss. I couldn't see Kathy's eyes, but I imagine she was recording parallel changes. Regina's look just seemed to open and open and open, as though she were receiving understanding without limit, as though she were finally seeing something for the first time, I have never seen her look so much a woman as at that moment, when she let herself be touched and loved by a woman, and could accept it with all its ambivalence and crashing beauty. Kathy made a sound deep in her throat and said, 'Yes, baby, yes.' And then Regina was in her arms, kissing her throat, moving her head down and lapping at her nipples. She took Kathy's breast in her mouth and sucked at it with enough energy to drain it dry. Her hands came up around Kathy's shoulders, and she lay back, drawing Kathy on top of her.

Kathy disengaged herself and let Regina lie there a long time, just watching her, and then she looked up at me. Some obscure warning bell went off in an untended corner of my mind, and my instinct was to continue sitting just where I was, but the sight of Regina stretched out like that, waiting, open, languorous, unnerved me. I scooted down and sat myself between her legs. Her cunt was copiously wet and little tremors made the insides of her thighs dance. My cock got hard at once, and completely silenced the clanging in my head. I leaned forward and lowered myself gently onto the waiting body.

The minute I entered her I knew it was wrong. It felt good to me, but she tensed immediately. All of a sudden my cock felt like a crude instrument, an ugly insensitive tool which had no business thrashing around such a fragile and almost other-worldly thing as a cunt. All the tales and horror stories concerning lesbians ran through my head: 'Once a woman has had another woman, she doesn't want a man,' and 'Once a woman has had a lesbian's tongue, she laughs at cocks,' and so on. I had, in my liberalism, dismissed all that as rubbish, and stoutly maintained that there was room enough in this universe for tongues and cocks, for lesbians and bisexuals. But now all my suppressed doubt hit at once, and I felt my cock beginning to go limp.

To my surprise, as soon as it was half-hard, Regina began to respond. Her cunt wrapped itself around the soft prick and started massaging it, comforting it, caressing it. It was all happening too fast and too heavy for me to come up with any formulations at the moment. It was a scrumptious feeling and I let my full weight fall on her. She spread her legs and brought up her knees so that

I fell comfortably into the cradle she made, and then she brought her hands to my face and began stroking me gently. I felt as though I were an infant, and part of me rebelled at this particular role, while the more sensible part told me to shut up and enjoy what was happening, whatever it was.

Regina moved with the caution of a mother holding a newborn infant. Her cunt was a thing of infinite subtlety. Its warmth and softness set me dreaming, and as I let myself slide into a formless reverie, my cock began to stiffen. But this time there was no *me* behind its action. It just engorged itself on blood and sensation, and filled up to its full hard stance. Yet, even in its hardness, there was an unusual quality of softness. I could feel the tip, and sensed the serrated edges of it kissing the tender secret inner parts of her pussy. I moved not at all, but let her do all the guiding.

Shortly my ears began to get heat flashes, and my face tingled, I could feel a trembling beginning in my legs and the breath came short and fast. Something was taking over my body and I let it happen. My shoulders shook and then my spine began to roll. Finally, my pelvis started to twitch back and forth very rapidly and in a few seconds my entire body was a crescendo of heat and movement. A long high cry came from my lips and Regina said, in a melting voice, over and over again, 'oh, oh, oh, oh, oh, oh, oh,' as the sperm rocketed up my cock and splashed into her cunt

104

in hot streaming jets, one after the other, coming out of the opening in rhythm to the convulsion spasms of my body. I came into her, and she received me wetly and darlingly.

I collapsed in her arms and we lay there for a long while, gently cradling one another. And then, as though from another planet, I felt a hand tapping me on the shoulder. Oh my God, it was Kathy! I had forgotten all about her. She flashed me an approving smile and then indicated, with a jerk of her thumb, that she wanted me to get off. Although I thought I should have been resentful, actually I wasn't. More puzzled than anything else.

I pulled back and rolled off to one side. Regina opened her eyes and looked up dazedly. She looked as though she had not the slightest idea of who or what anything or anyone was at the moment. But before she could stir, Kathy was down on her. She went with the rapidity and and grace of a boa snaring a lamb. I watched as her still smiling lips, curved like a scimitar, cut into the pulsing, slippery lips of Regina's cunt. And then her mouth covered the hole, and I lost sight of all the details.

At first Regina stiffened, and her hands come down to the top of Kathy's head, as they have so often since come down on mine at such a moment. It was an indication that she would let herself be eaten, but she wanted to keep control on the parameters of the experience. Kathy merely shook her head from side to side and brushed the hands off. She did it with such finality and sense of authority that Regina whimpered and brought her hands up to her chest, where, tentatively, and then with greater purpose, she began to flick her nipples and massage her own breasts.

Kathy dropped her head down and Regina parted her legs even more, bringing her cunt up. Kathy's tongue slithered out and plunged into the cunt hole. Regina shuddered and I leaned forward, mesmerised by the action. Kathy worked quickly and directly, forcing her face deeper, getting Regina's cunt to spread wider, until, all at once, Regina brought her legs up and caught them behind the knees with her hands to hold them high and spread. Her ass came into sight and Kathy's right hand moved between the cheeks. I couldn't see what her fingers were doing, since they were hidden by her face, but now Regina began to moan, deep chesty sobs that were ragged at the edges and described a feeling that she had probably never experienced before. It was the sound of a woman who was about to come. Kathy dug in more deeply and tried to catch the tide of passion as it reached its peak, but her move was too sudden and Regina's moans suddenly changed to gasps, a sort of retching sound such as a baby might make if it were choking on its milk. Her legs tightened and her hands came down again to push at Kathy's head. Part of me was dismayed but part of me smiled. If a woman couldn't get her to come, I didn't have to feel so bad.

But that was only round one. With infinite patience Kathy began again. This time she moved higher and her mouth opened and came back, only to be lowered over Regina's upper cunt, and I saw her curved tongue dip down to flick right at the tip of Regina's clitoris. This time the response was a frantic machine-gun burst of expelled breath. Kathy pulled back and came down again, this time licking from the bottom of the slit, right above the asshole, all the way up between the dripping lips, right up to the clitoris and into her pubic hair. She did this countless times, lapping at the cunt with great broad strokes, each time letting her tongue sink deeper into the crack as she licked her way up. Finally, Regina was again lying back, her legs in the air, letting her cunt fall out, while Kathy ravaged it at will. This time nipping at it with her teeth, and growling into the hole, and teasing the tiny clitoris with the tip of her tongue. Regina shuddered and moaned, and once again stopped the flow, this time by clamping her legs together. 'It's too much,' she said. 'Not enough!' I said in my head, echoing Ivan the Terrible.

Kathy took a deep breath and forcibly brought Regina's legs apart. She had a determined gleam in her eye. Up to now it had been sport and play; but I could see the pride of the professional being challenged. I recognised it easily. Many a time I

107

had fucked with my awareness on the technical specifics of the act as opposed to the so-called human relationship. Kathy leaned forward and into the space between Regina's thighs. Now she brought her right hand up and inserted three fingers into Regina's sticky twat. Her hand went in up to the knuckles and then her mouth came down to cover the upper lips. And now a long struggle and ride ensued.

Regina came again and again to the very peak off orgasm, but Kathy was hipper to her rhythms this time, and before Regina had a chance to cut off the flow, Kathy pulled back a short distance, leaving her hanging there. Then Kathy remained perfectly still and waited for her to begin the next wave of movement. And Regina would, by relaxing her legs and belly, and letting her cunt sink even more deeply onto Kathy's fingers. I looked away from the confrontation between mouth and cunt and saw that Kathy's ass was high in the air and moving in short jerks up and down. My erection returned and began to throb. I wasn't sure if the move was politic or not, but I moved behind Kathy, only to see her cunt gaping full wide and dribbling like a child eating gruel. She was incredibly hot, and without hesitation, I came up close and slid my cock into the hole. She quivered and let out a low moan into Regina's cunt, while Regina in turn responded to that by pushing her pelvis up, thrusting her cunt further onto Kathy's fingers. The heat of the box, and the sight of the two women making it together with such fullness and beauty inflamed me to the point past control. I was in her for no more than a minute before I felt myself coming. I let out a cry and Regina opened her eyes, and as I shot my load into Kathy's waiting cunt, Regina and I looked deep into one another's eyes and passed messages that defied all conscious understanding.

I fell back and sat down. With the added impetus, Kathy really went at it. She was now all sinuosity and style. The game was out in the open. Regina would put up wall after wall of defence, challenging her lover to scale the gate and find her secret garden. Kathy was letting her know that the secret garden would be overgrown with weeds before long unless Regina was ready to at least take the barbed wire off the walls. And now Regina lay there, unable to pretend that I wasn't there, having Kathy consciously work at her cunt to make her come. She grew frantic, and her very nervousness provided the key. For now the energy began to course through her legs. She opened and clenched her hands, making and unmaking fits. She begged for mercy in a dozen silent ways.

But the mouth was ruthless. Kathy had now grown very expert in the ways of Regina's cunt. The retreats were fewer and lasted less time. Regina squirmed and her ass moved back and forth along the damp sheet under her. Kathy's mouth dripped saliva and cunt juice and sperm. Her hair was wild and plastered down her shoulders and on Regina's thighs. Regina's breasts jiggled from side to side as her nipples grew hard and gnarled. Her legs spread apart involuntarily, and her cries became deeper and fuller.

Finally she began a long slow ride to climax. Her belly went full and relaxed. Her arms lay out at her sides. She let herself be open, be vulnerable. The last gremlin in her cunt tried one last effort to break the rhythm, but Kathy moved in and with an expert twist of her fingers and luscious gobbling with her lips, took Regina right to the very edge, and then sweeping her up in her arms, dove over the precipice with her. And Regina let out a long loud cry that must have been heard down the entire block, a cry of relief and revelation, a beautiful joyous painful cry that saturated the room with sound and filled my heart with awe. And simultaneously Kathy sobbed and sobbed, sucking and sucking at the now throbbing, gushing cunt that pumped into her mouth the juice and vibration and love that it had worked so hard for.

Regina lay back and totally collapsed. Kathy lay with her face between her thighs for a good while. Then she pulled herself back and sat up. She turned around and looked at me, like a doctor who had just completed a long, difficult, successful operation. She was tired, drawn, and totally fulfilled. I filled with admiration and warmth for her, and in a gesture that might have seemed the height of the ridiculous, I reached forward and shook her hand. 'Congratulations,' I said with my eyes. 'Thanks,' she smiled back at me.

We grinned at one another like fools, and in that instant I found the sister I had been searching for all my life. There would never be misunderstanding between us again.

Regina roused herself and sat up. She looked like the little girl who had fallen asleep at the picnic and now rubbed her eyes, questioning whether it was time to go home. Now Kathy and I became father and mother. We both moved over and took Regina in our arms. And suddenly, all roles dropped. We were one.

Now the astonishment reached us, the sense of what it was that just happened. With all the games aside, all the hidden motivations, all the grotesque posturings and silly social roles, the fact was that Regina had had her first orgasm. And that I had known a kind of fucking I didn't imagine was possible. And Kathy had made peace with her desire for women in the eyes of a man. All of us, in a very important way, had moved a great step forward in maturity and self-understanding. And we had broken the taboo, the taboo of two.

Three was not only possible, it was desirable, and perhaps superior. Of course, that was the first flash, and in the weeks afterwards, when we tried living together, we found that while three brings greater joy and fuller understanding, it also makes the stakes higher on the pain and suspicion side. And the games got heavy, with Regina attempting to seduce me away from Kathy, and Kathy trying to cut me out from Regina, and me trying to dig each of them independently and yet manipulating things in such a way as to have them together. After a month we were at one another's throats, and began arguing over ugly things, like money responsibility, and housework sharing, and time allocation.

We finally split up, going in three different directions. Yet for all the shit which came afterwards, there were times of unalloyed bliss, times when we fucked like one organism, when there was no one doing anything to anyone but all of us pouring ourselves into a common centre from which we all took bounty. I was very comfortable with Regina then, because she didn't look to me for all her needs, and Kathy gave her an emotional fulfillment that I couldn't. Kathy and I became as close as brother and sister, now free to swap stories and feelings, talking about our lovers, male and female, me coming to terms with the ways I played subtle roles to cover up the fact of my homosexual feelings, and playing the mind-bending game of fucking men in order to deny how much I wanted to fuck men.

We developed a small ritual of holding hands in a circle before eating dinner. The sense of dusk, of good food on the table, of peace settling over the house after the busy day, of the lush evening about to begin, is always with me. And even now, whenever Regina and I sit down to dinner, we hold hands, her left in my right, and we look to the empty spot where Kathy once sat, wondering whether some day the three of us might not be together again, in some way, for some reason.

But at this moment Kathy is down the California coast, attempting to become an encounter group leader, and fighting the battle between her need of the experience and her subtle cynicism which understands the process as the palliative of our time. And Regina waits for me in Mendocino, in her country home, surrounded by the timid hip and semi-retired of the California middle class. And I long for more adventure, the freedom of wild travel to inner worlds and outer countries.

The phone rang, It was Roy, a sometime lover I met at the Baths a few months ago. He had some poppers and a few friends who wanted to have an orgy. 'Maybe Friday,' he said. 'Could be,' I said. I had lost his number, and as he gave it to me, I noticed that I wrote it on the back of the envelope which contained Regina's letter. She seemed far distant, too removed even for jealousy.

(6)

I DO NOT know of one successful marriage. This used to be strange until I realised that I do not know one successful human being. The mark of the species is imperfection. And all attempts at improvement end in a more subtle, or a more brutal, form of tyranny. From the earliest moments of existence the poison works its influence. A mother's anger changes the chemistry of the bloodstream, and the unsuspecting foetus in her belly receives its first negative conditioning. The time before birth is a school for survival, and the first lesson taught is selectivity.

Then we come gasping into the world, and are met with duplicity, sterility, hatred, confusion, war, disease, cosmic indifference, and the enigma of being. And all the while we are processed by parents, by priests, by teachers, by political leaders, by the men who write the books we read, who make the art, who inscribe the philosophies. And rarely, if ever, do we meet a human being whose only interest in us is seeing that we grow naturally, that we develop fully. No, all those who come into our lives have expectations, needs, prejudices, and so we are shaped and misformed, counting ourselves lucky if we reach maturity without some fatal trauma having radically warped our sense of life.

And with all this, two people come together in this thing called marriage and agree that it shall be different for their children. And of course it never is.

I looked at the letter Regina sent, the letter which, like all the others, calls me to her, asks me to join her in the plot of making a home. We stand naked before each other, our weaknesses and fears, our treachery and instability, all revealed. And we wonder whether our consciousness of how we are made is enough to free us from the trap. I have often thought that consciousness of the condition somehow freed me from that condition, and with that excused all my essays into degeneracy. Until the night I woke up, as it were, in the middle of a vile orgy, with people who were mostly drunk, and whose sense of sexuality rose no higher than a mindless slobbering over anonymous bodies. Although it seemed out of place, I

118

managed a wry smile upon realising that awareness is illusory frosting on the cake, that what
is, and who I *am*, so immensely pervades and
overshadows my understanding of it, that I fooled
myself to think that cynical detachment somehow
made me 'better' than the situation in which I
found myself.

With that last bastion of security destroyed, I
have since wandered in a land without markers,
not knowing how to judge any action or thought,
and so resolved simply to let myself move spontaneously, and not to consider the intricacies of
style or content. Yet that led me straight to dissi-
pation, and within myself I became conservative,
the final refuge of the aging coward. Two nights
later, I called Roy. The tension concerning my
decision of going to the Coast, to set up house
with Regina and the nightmare suspicion that I
was plunging headlong into a self-destructive contract which would activate all the reactive modes
of my personality, had me on the ropes. Perhaps
I felt by this act of going to Roy's that I could
at least temporarily see myself. Perhaps I had a
burning need deep in my bowels and wanted cock.

I walked over to the West Village, filled with
thoughts of deception. In a sense I was betraying
my trust to Regina, but I felt no betrayal within
myself; the only treason came if I considered her
in relation to what was happening, But what was
happening didn't concern her, except by her defi-
nition. This got to the core of my resentment: I

was fine until her frame of reference got grafted onto my eyes. That was the very trap I didn't want to succumb to. And by the time I reached Roy's door, a swaggering sense of bravado propelled me into the house.

He was there, dressed in a shirt which came to just below his cock, and nothing else on. The lights were very low, and I could hear voices in the next room. A thrill of heavy anticipation ran through my balls and I felt my ass tingle. Whatever the psychology of the situation might have been, the straight biological lesson was clear: I got something from making it with men that just didn't happen with women. And there was no one in all of creation who could tell me it was a perversion or a sickness. My motives might have been awry, but the simple act of homosexual fucking was as right as anything a man and women did together. I smelled orgy in the air, and Roy smiled at me, his teeth gleaming between his black lips as he said 'Hello' in his strong West Indian accent.

'Some friends of mine came over,' he continued. 'Come in and meet them.' I followed him into the living room, a small New York parody on the name, barely large enough to accommodate the five people now in it. The introductions went around: John, Paul, George. It was a mixed bag. John was a hulking narcissist, almost six feet two, with a thrust of dirty blonde hair and a perpetual pose in his posture. He looked over at me

120

in that odd way they have, suggesting that the only proper relation was the way in which I would worshipfully look at him. Paul was a queen in men's clothing. He was one of those super-soft black boys who look as though they spent the first sixteen years of life on mama's tit. Great pendulous lips and soft liquid eyes, his skin shone with a dull glow and his ass rose provocatively in a high tight curve through his clinging white pants. George looked like a librarian, with an indeterminate face. He could have been anywhere from twenty-five to forty years old, and had a certain faded quality about him, like a piece of driftwood that has been in the sun a long time.

I sat down, took a proffered beer, and joined the party. It was at the small-talk stage, tales of last year on Fire Island, gossip about the raids in the local gay bars. There were issues of *Screw* and *Gay* strewn about. Within half an hour or so I would be involved with these men in a groaning tangle of bodies, with cocks and asses and fantasies open full blast, and all of us sucking and fucking and diving in and out of whatever forms of sexual excitement we dug, and yet here we were, indulging in inane chitchat, without any warmth or true humour or eye contact. We were like soldiers about to attack an enemy fortification, making small talk to cover our nervousness, or to give some social pretext to delay our readiness. Men don't seem to need as much foreplay as women.

Roy stood up. 'Why don't we go make ourselves

comfortable,' he said. We all looked at one another, sized up one another's bodies and took a fix on the flesh, and headed for the bedroom. This was a different affair, bigger than the living room, and consisting mostly of two huge mattresses laid side by side on the floor. A red light made the room nicely suggestive. And one wall was a set of full-length mirrors. We filed in, hesitated for a moment, and without further ado, began taking off our clothes. There was something of the locker room about the activity, and part of me resented the stereotypic nature of the scene. Yet I realised that acting out one drama was as valid as any other, and elegance had so often got in the way of utility that I could appreciate the briskness of this approach. As we dropped our pants and took off our shirts, we exchanged more or less surreptitious glances, measuring the sizes of cocks and looking at how the asses hung.

Then we were nude. Paul fell forward and lay on his back on the mattress, squirming a little and stretching luxuriously. John struck a magazine cover pose against the wall, leaning his torso back and pulling on his cock with his right hand. For a moment I smirked at the silliness of the posture, but then an old familiar weakness made my knees go slack and I felt a pressure in my chest. His cock grew hard and bulged out from the pubic hair, thick and mean. His balls hung like oat sacks underneath. I found myself moving over toward him, mesmerised by the tool. I looked into his eyes and met the cool disdain with which he meets all men, the knowledge that the sheer presence of his body is enough to get men to suck him off and let themselves be fucked. I stood in front of him, and then sank heavily to my knees. The cock shot straight up before me, throbbing slightly. The purple tip contrasted with the pale white shaft. For a long while I drank it in with my eyes, feasting myself on the weight and succulence of it. Then, trembling and unable to bear the tension any longer, I leaned my head forward, and with a sob took the velvety lush knob in my mouth. My mouth was dry and his cock rasped against my lips. I licked the tip of his cock with my tongue and wet it. I pulled back and plunged forward again, this time using my tongue like a washcloth, lapping the cock all over, covering it with saliva, making it slippery. He drew in his breath with short hisses and put his hand on the top of my head, giving me gentle pressure to go even more forward. I took a deep breath, closed my eyes, and then began the long slow descent on the entire shaft, feeling it go past my teeth, over my tongue and to the back of my mouth. I relaxed deep in my jaw and then let the immense prick slide into my throat, making the opening very wide, deeper, until it lodged down almost to my adam's apple. I felt myself heaving from deep in my stomach, and as my body convulsed, my throat tightened its grip on the head of his cock. He groaned and his knees buckled. As much as I was able, I smiled to myself; I had been able to blow his cool as well as his cock.

I pulled back and felt his cock make the reverse journey as my throat snapped shut behind it, and it slithered up my tongue to my lips, where I kissed the tip of it tenderly, loving it with my tongue.

I moved back and lay on the mattress. Right behind me Paul was lying on his stomach, his mouth stretched tight around Roy's cock. He worked with that quick feverish corkscrew motion that many cocksuckers affect, but which has always left me cold. I prefer long-drawn-out affairs where the entire mouth and throat become totally sensitive and actually communicate with the cock. Of course, I get into frenzies also, but they come as the culmination of a long preparation of slow sucking. George was lying behind Paul, his face buried in the large black buttocks. He had the cheeks pried apart with his hands, and his tongue worked up and down the entire crack of Paul's ass. Paul wriggled and pushed his ass back, and with a gulping sound George thrust his tongue forcibly and wetly into his asshole. He slobbered like a dog with a new bone.

John came forward and knelt on the bed between my legs. He looked down at me sternly, and despite myself, I felt my limbs grow heavy. He moved up until his knees were prying my thighs apart and then he reached down and pulled my legs up and placed my ankles over his shoulders. My ass was all the way up off the bed and exposed to his menacing cock. 'Some jelly,' I said, hoping for lubricant. But he just looked down at my ass, spread the cheeks apart, and brought his rod up into the crack. I was dry and tight, not having had a man for weeks. He put his fingers in my mouth and I covered them with saliva, which he then brought down to rub on the tip of his cock. Slowly the large engine slid toward the tiny opening, and when it nudged right at the hole, I shuddered and let all my tension go. I was his, no matter what he did. I was open and vulnerable, and all I wanted was to feel that hot gnarled prick move its way into my bowels.

I felt it break in, and for a moment it seemed that I was losing my virginity all over again. A sharp spasm went through my middle and I caught my breath. He wasn't cruel and didn't push in hard; but he wasn't kind, so the steady intrusion continued. The expression on his face hadn't changed. It was the trancelike solemnity of an anaesthetist putting the mask over someone's face. I didn't know whether he was experiencing pleasure in his cock or not; his entire attention seemed focused on me and my reactions. I let my legs fall back and reached down to spread my cheeks further, to pull the membrane of my asshole back so that he didn't pull on it as he entered. He went deeper and deeper until he was all the way inside. I felt the end of him as a dull, sweet ache deep inside me. And from that point all else flowed.

Then he melted and swooped down on me. His mouth found mine and to my surprise, his lips were gentle and sensitive. All the hard lines in his face melted, and suddenly he seemed very young, no more than a teenager. His beautiful cock worked its will inside me and I loved it with everything I had. I brought my ass up and forward so he could penetrate more deeply. I ran my hands up and down his back, feeling the strength in his shoulders, the smooth skin sloping down past his spine to his ass, which contracted and released as he pumped his pelvis into me. He was, for that moment, for all that, my darling. I became a total woman for him, letting him see me, letting him know me, letting him go into the heart of me. I saw myself, lying wantonly beneath his rippling body, my legs wrapped completely around him, as I fondled his ears and kissed his throat, making deep murmuring sounds into his chest. For a few minutes we were as one, feeling and relating to nothing else but the fires of our own passion, absolutely lost in one another. Then I felt him begin to grow deeply excited and I knew he was about to come. 'Do it,' I whispered, 'come inside me, give it to me now, fuck it all inside me.'

But at that point, he stopped. He froze his pelvis tight and strangled the sperm welling up through his tube. He lay perfectly still for a moment and then slowly pulled out. All the softness had gone and he was back in costume again. His cock came out hard and tough and there was sense of disappointment and disgust that ran through me. The bastard had been stingy, and wanted to save his load for later. But just then a deep, exalted relaxation swept through my body. I sank and wriggled down deeper into the mattress, wanting to be covered, wanting to be touched, wanting to be overpowered. John came forward and knelt by my head, his knees at my shoulders. The cock sang over me, and with a sigh, I reached up to lick it. But he grabbed my hair and held my head back. I whimpered and tried harder to get his cock. He pulled my head back hard to the mattress. Suddenly I was inflamed with desire. More than anything I had to have that incredible piece of meat in my mouth. 'Please,' I said, 'please.' He looked down. 'Please what?' he hissed. 'Let me have it, let me suck you off, please put it in my mouth,' I moaned. He smiled thinly and bent forward, bringing the cock to my lips. I opened my mouth wide and put my tongue up to lick the tiny slit in the head of his prick. he put all his weight on me, and all of a sudden his cock came rushing into my mouth, hard and fast. I gasped for breath but he didn't give me a chance. He kept my hair pulled back and began to grind his tool deep into me, bruising my throat. He worked it all over the inside of my mouth, into my cheeks and along the roof of my mouth and again and again past my throat opening and down as far as he could reach into my gullet.

Just then I felt my legs being lifted again. Roy moved in and, to my relief, smeared KY down the crack and into my asshole. Then without further preliminaries he sank his cock into my already used ass. I took it with a grunt, and simultaneously felt the cock in my mouth sink deeper. Then they began working in unison. I heard Paul, who had come to lie beside me, crooning, 'Oh fuck him, baby, fuck him good.' And then he moved his hand over to begin pinching my nipples hard. My ass loosened even more, and then I was past any point of tension. I was all openness and wet and heat. I lay back and wailed. My ass was wide open, spread apart and sucking in the cock that rammed again and again into the deepest part of me. I was making gurgling, sloshing sounds in my throat, and writhing under the punishment of Paul's hands. I sailed off into the wild abandon I so much cherish, where all the fantasies swell into great archetypal images dancing in an immense round to a silent music. I became all men and all women, all life and all death, all mortality and all eternity. I drew in the vibrant male energy pumping into me, sucking at pleasure and meaning, draining them of all their vibrations. I heard myself crying and singing long loud high notes.

And then I descended back to the bedroom, feeling the grunting groaning bodies working their way into me. Spasms had begun to shake Roy, and in a moment he pumped harder and harder into my ass. 'You bitch,' he cried, 'you fucking bitch,' as he slapped my ass and pinched my thighs. I welcomed it all, all the abuse and all the emotion. Let him let it all out, I thought, let it all pour into me, because I'm hungry and thirsty and I need psychic blood, I need what I drain from these fools who imagine that sex has to do only with what happens between genitals. The vampire in me rose high, and with a great shriek dragged the vital spark from their bodies. Roy ducked and slammed full and deep into my ass. And at almost the same time, John's enormous cock lodged itself deep in my throat, unbudgingly, and spewed jet after jet of sperm down into my chest. I drank it all in and let myself fall off the edge of the precipice.

For a long, long time it was all quiet, and then the cock in my mouth grew limp and slithered out from between my lips, leaving a thin line of sperm over my chin. Roy pulled his cock out and my ass fell limp on the sheet, my legs lying as though broken. They moved back and I prepared to sit up. But I had forgotten Paul and George.

George rolled me over on my stomach and suddenly I felt very naked and very exposed with my ass up in the air. And then the first blow came, a stinging slap across my buttocks with a thick flat belt. I grabbed the sheet in my fists and bit the pillow. Again the strap came down. Each time it hit, the reddening cheeks felt it more. Almost to my surprise I found myself lifting my ass up to receive the blows faster and fuller. 'Look, the little queen likes it,' I heard someone say, and was astonished to consider that they were talking about me. Who I was in terms of my personality had long since disappeared; all that was left was this organism that for some reason enjoyed the extremities of pain and pleasure.

Then they were all on me at once. Paul rolled me over and sat on my face. The deep musky smell of the space between his thighs, the dark spot between the balls and asshole, overpowered me and I sank into it. I began licking and slobbering all up and down the tender centre of his sex. He moved forward and I felt the pinched membrane of his asshole rub harshly against my mouth. I became a mindless lapping animal, grovelling and sucking. Then someone grabbed my balls and began squeezing. I cried out but when I opened my mouth, Paul's ass only smothered me more. Someone was pinching at my nipples again and slapping at my belly. I was totally in their power and wanted to be nowhere else.

A period of total confusion followed. I was all at once smothered in bodies and the same people who had been punishing me were now licking me and kissing me, running their hands tenderly up and down my body. George put his mouth over my cock and began sucking it with all the gentleness in the world. I felt myself melt and started whimpering like a little girl lost. This inflamed them more and George pulled back, and with a cry of 'Oh baby,' leaned forward and brought his cock to my ass. I desired him then more than I can remember wanting anything in my life. 'Oh fuck me,' I cried and opened my legs to him. he sank into me easily and warmly, and his large soft cock filled me with delight and longing. I brought my ass up to get as close to him as I could, and then holding on tightly, let him ride and ride and ride. He moved with a great joy and spirit, not holding anything back, letting himself feel me, letting himself feel himself. I felt the orgasm welling up in him long before there was any physical sign of it; it was a kind of distant rumbling like the sound of surf from far away. I let the entire inside of me go loose and pushed out, opening to draw him in. He sank into me further and began sobbing in my ear, 'Oh baby, darling, yes baby, yes.' And then, from deep under his cock, the spasms began and I could feel the sperm shooting up the soft underbelly of his tool, as load after load lodged itself deep in my ass. I held him tightly and felt his cock throb for a long time afterward, and then slowly, gently, felt him go limp and slide out.

After that, suddenly, it was over for me. Roy began to make a move toward me, but I cut it off. I felt satisfied and wanted no more. Or so I thought. It was that point when, in fucking women, I generally get frustrated if they have had sufficient and I have yet to come. I fell back on the bed protesting, but he deftly reached down and put his finger in my ass. At once, all resistance melted. I had flip-flopped from refusal to acceptance in the blink of an eye. He rolled me over on my stomach and spread my cheeks apart. Once again I sank into a heavy bliss, and felt a cock move inside me. I began to feel insatiable, as though I could let myself get fucked again and again forever, never wanting to be without it, never wanting to feel an empty hole where there could be a fullness entering it.

I moved up on my knees, put my head on the sheet, and let myself relax. I felt like doing nothing, like not responding at all, just letting the delicious cock work its wonderful ride into me. I slipped into a kind of haze where nothing existed except the fact of my ass exposed to anyone who wanted to fuck me. Paul pulled out and I felt a movement behind me, and another cock came in. I didn't know which of them it was, but let him fuck me as much as he wanted.

I don't know how long it lasted or which of them fucked me for how long. I didn't care, I was all ass, all invitation. Someone came, and then someone else fucked me, and he came, and then a third person fucked me, and he came, I was sore and dribbling, but ready for it to go on forever.

And then it stopped. I looked back and saw the four of them standing up next to the mattress. I slid forward and rolled over. I felt juicy and tropical. And then they grabbed my legs and began pulling me. I didn't know what they were doing. They grabbed me under my shoulders and lifted, and the four of them carried me to the bathroom.

More than anything else I felt peace, a great pervading calm that reached to the outermost edges of the universe. Whatever demons had been haunting me were now either driven off or appeased, and I was totally my own person again.

As I climbed up out of the tub I smiled a private smile to myself. I was still a Catholic, expiating my sins through some form of communion. But this came closer to what a group of decadent witches might do than anything that ever happened in St Patrick's Cathedral. No wonder church attendance is falling off, I thought. They don't know how to put on a good show anymore.

This was one of my crazy moments, when I was free of all context. I could see all the historical postures and social roles, and how I played them and who I was in relation to them, but none of them was me. *Me* was the flow, the movement, the unformed being which constantly gives life to manifestations. *Me* was life, and life has no labels.

I showered and then went out. They were back on the mattress, still naked. I had had enough for the night so I bade them farewell. Roy made a halfhearted effort to get me to stay, but I wasn't being seduced this time. I dressed, had a cigarette with them as we lapsed again into a kind of small talk. But this time the words had a glow to them, and there was more eye contact than could be assimilated. It was an exquisitely intimate impersonal moment.

I left and we all made vague assurances that we would 'do it again sometime.' I realised that sooner or later, one way or another, we would.

As I walked back to my apartment, I felt as though I were floating off the ground. It was a kind of elation that I never get after fucking women, and then I realised the difference. With women, I am drained; I lapse into an easy sleep to regain my energies, and I feel relaxed and cozy. But when I take it from a man, I am the one who sucks in the energy, and afterwards there is a quiet glow which burns in me like the embers after a well-made fire.

There was a further consideration. After fucking with a man, I feel totally free afterwards. We enjoy one another, can be tender and loving, or bad and hurting, but when it is over, it is over. We each return to our separate selves and are able to make an easy transition to a state without immediate touch. But with women there enters a kind of cloying quality, a sense of possession, a feeling that they have somehow lodged a hook in me, and no matter what I do they have a line to draw me back in.

Some of that is my neurotic fear of being swallowed by the mother figure, but at least half of it is an objective condition. Perhaps it is because women are conditioned to be dependent, or perhaps it is the manifestation of a biological need in them to hold on to the man they are fucking, as though he were a mate, someone to protect the home and help rear the children. It occurred to me that either we should be back in a situation where everyone lived in small villages, or else the problem of promiscuity would continue to haunt us. If, underneath all the sophistication, women were still zoologically imprinted to making it with one man, then the whole sexual freedom scene was a flatulent lie, the construction of horny men and confused women.

My thoughts raced back to Regina again. No matter what else happened, I knew that I would have to have the kind of scene I had just been in, it was as important to me as my morning meditation. But could she share in it? And if so, how? And if she couldn't, then we would be back in the old bind where the woman sits at home with a candle in the window or has secret lovers, while her old man goes chasing his aberrant sexual desires.

I felt very clean about my relationship with Regina just then. The problem stood out in clear relief, and while no easy solution offered itself, for the first time in weeks I didn't feel tortured.

(7)

MEANING IS SIMPLY a question of finding the correspondences between different-sized infinities. The trouble with Aristotle's notion of identity is that he had no understanding of scale. One line can be longer than another, but they contain the same number of points.

I am struck by the uncanny resemblance between words and life. When a description is accurate, it configures the past, confirms the present, and outlines the future, all in one stroke. There is nothing more damaging than badly-used language. This is what makes writing so difficult. The line of prose or poetry, if it is to be true, must capture the energy of the moment, no matter what the ideational content of the words. But when that happens, there is no discernible difference between the fiction and the reality. Symbol blends with stuff, and all is clear. As a friend of mind once remarked, 'Yin and yang – what a terribly complex way to look at things.'

On the floor lay the letter from Regina. I took out the sheet and stared at the words on the page. Two nights ago it had been a living experience; now the typewritten letters seemed oddly stilted, and I was unable to read a word. On the envelope was scrawled a telephone number. I realised with a mild shock that it was Roy's number. The orgy swam into my memory with all the psychic distance of a movie. Unreal, everything was unreal. Abruptly, I walked over to the typewriter, rolled in a sheet of paper, and began writing.

'Regina: For whatever reasons, the way I approach the problems of living is through defining my own reality as it occurs to me, without pressure from any other human being to meet any standards whatsoever. I am here, now, as close as I can be to that energy which seems to pervade all life at its most honest and peaceful moments. I have only a vague notion of the form my life will take.

'As far as I can see marriage is a death sentence to the soul. Which doesn't mean that living without marriage is any more real or facile. For me to uproot myself to come live in Lotusland by the ironic Pacific would be a masterstroke of idiocy.

140

There is no impulse at all in me to come there, so I am staying here.

'The question of our relationship is again wide open. I will be in touch with you, and you will know where I'm at. If at any time it seems that you want to come join me, you will know who it is you are coming to be with. I am not going to change myself in the slightest to accommodate any of your needs, and I don't expect you to accommodate yourself to me.

'When I am in your area, I will come be with you. Until then, I think of the words in the Baez song you had me listen to, and the stars that shine in your sky are the same that shine in mine.'

I signed it, put it in an envelope, addressed and stamped it, and put it by the door so I would remember to mail it. I had a sudden ferocious sense of liberation. I was my own man again. The thought of Regina shot through me like a pang, and I clutched at my chest, and then it passed. I would miss her sharply. But I felt that never before had we had a better chance of succeeding.

There was something extremely literary about the moment. I had disposed of a human being through a letter, as though she were a character in a novel. And to my astonishment, I realised that that was how I felt to myself. I suddenly saw my entire life as a more or less absurd odyssey of a cunning cocksman being ensnared by numberless adventures and almost going to ruin between the rocks of lust and metaphysics. But who was the faithful wife to whom I was trying to return? Was Regina Penelope? Again the literary myth! My head started to dance.

There was nothing for it. I went to the phone and called California. I had to talk to her, at least to her voice, so that some palpable reality would intrude onto this diabolical trampoline which had me in thrall. I didn't mind the bouncing up and down, but I couldn't abide the notion that I was doing my act in an empty theatre on a deserted world. The phone rang twice and she answered. I realised at once, as my heart gladdened, that what I loved her for most was that she was always right there when I needed her. 'Hello,' I said. There was the usual pause, and then she whispered, warmly, 'Hi.'

'I called for two reasons,' I said. 'One is to make sure that you are real, and I suppose, by that, to make sure that I am real. And the other is to give you a brush-off. I'm not coming to California.'

A silence. Then, 'Ever?' 'Not for a while,' I said. 'At least not the next four months.' I heard her exhale deeply. 'Oh, that's too bad,' she said, 'but I was afraid for a minute that you weren't coming at all.' The thought went through my mind, 'Maybe I'm not,' but I blanked it out before it registered. 'I wrote you a letter,' I said. 'You want to hear it?' She said yes and I got the letter and read it to her. She didn't say anything for a while, and then, 'I'm all confused again.'

'It's pretty clear,' I said. 'Coming to live with you is not important enough to me to take me away from what I am doing here right now. And I won't make any promises about the future.' She began to counter what I said in the subtle way she has which makes it seem as though we are arguing some negotiable point instead of talking about a decision which has been made. She seemed so vulnerable at that moment that my heart went out to her. For a brief second my resolve wavered, but I snapped back into a firm posture. I pictured her standing there nude, her ass a panorama of shifting tints and textures, her eyes doing a seductive dance, her sweet curly cunt hair peeking at me from between her legs. And I realised I was closing access to all that.

But not to her! Then I saw the difference. All of my problems concerning my feelings about Regina centred around sexual access, and jealousy, and fear that she would find a groovier cock. But as far as the woman, the person, was concerned, I felt an easy affection and warmth; I cared for her, suffered with her, shared joy with her. And the fact that I couldn't fuck her and somebody else would, had nothing to do with whether I loved her or not. Fucking was a form of loving, but no more so than talking, or holding, or working with, or sharing silence with. The twin emotions of sadness and release sloshed around in my chest like green water in a bottle. If I were with Regina right now, I should laugh with her, and take her in my arms, and while I told her all of the joyous bubbling insanity in my mind, I would fuck her tenderly and roughly with my body.

Yet she was not with me physically, and the words had become a substitute for touch instead of just another part of the dance. I told her that I didn't want to talk any more because any further conversation would just make us muddled and resentful. She agreed, and promising to write and call one another soon, we hung up.

I was very excited. She had spent most of her time telling me how much I turned her on when I was this way, but being this way meant our separation. We seemed caught in that not uncommon trap of desiring in proportion to distance. Sharing the same bed was too close; three thousand miles was too far. I wondered what the ideal geographic space was for a sane marriage between man and woman. Paradoxically, I felt that our marriage was stronger than it had been before I told her I wouldn't be joining her, and before she acknowledged that she would probably now be fucking some of the men she'd flashed over the past few weeks.

Just then the phone rang. It was Michael, inviting me to spend a few days in the country with his wife and children. It seemed perfect timing, so I accepted at once and made preparations to meet him at the bus station. I showered, dressed, and headed for Port Authority Bus Terminal. Within an hour, he was driving up to greet me.

Michael is a psychiatrist about thirty-five years old. He is successful, handsome, hip, and very intelligent. But like all of us, his brightness doesn't extend to those areas where he has a vested interest in not looking. He is married to a statuesque European, and after seven years they have three children on an acre of ground in a solid, graceful, three-story wood house. Whereas some men allow the child and teenager to predominate to the detriment of the adult in them, Michael is almost one-hundred-percent adult all the time, which becomes overpowering. She is as heavy in the head as he is, and they look as though they fuck magnificently. He is well over six feet and has a kind of bullish physique which is still delicate; she is a few inches shorter, with breasts that would each fill a large hand, and the kind of trim, functional ass which seems as though it knows exactly how to move. A mordant mouth provides the cherry on top of the sexual pie. Each time I saw her, I itched to see her cunt.

He and I have a friendship that started from the moment we saw one another. Total mutual respect and liking have been its unfailing characteristics. His problems with Ina are classic. His passion is his work and the people who constitute that work. She is burdened by her housework and children, and her sense of being left out of the mainstream of his life. She can't share his scene, or won't. So they stay together for the sake of comfort, and play incredible games with one

145

another with the full arsenal of spitefulness and seduction. They have tried swinging and three-somes and various forms of sexual escapades, but none of them worked because their basic bond is shattered. The energy doesn't flow fully between them any longer.

I arrived and immediately began spreading good will all over the place, digging the kids in a special way, and laying non-threatening sex vibes on Ina, and getting the whole scene cool with Michael. We rapped, and did a settling down number, and had dinner, and then went to sit around the fireplace to smoke grass and talk. From experience in this kind of scene, I knew that nothing worthwhile would happen among us unless the totality of the drama was exposed. So I drew the scenario for them. Jealous but bored husband feeling guilty about his wife invites good friends up to make love to her, with or without him present, in the hopes of rejuvenating his scene with her. Bitchy wife refusing to even find out how she feels for fear that knowledge might force her to discard her mask of hatefulness. And the galloping guru trying to put all the angles together to find the proper-shaped triangle. Usually husband and wife make up about one hundred and fifty degrees between them, leaving the third in the menage to juggle with forty, a narrow margin. And no matter what happens, unless everyone understands his angle, and knows that the degree

146

of the angle is always subject to change, there will be trouble among the concerned parties.

By the time I had brought my narrative up to the reality, which was the three of us sitting there in the middle of this insane suburban melodrama, they were ready to cop, and smiled at the absurdity of our condition. And for the first time a look of warmth passed between them. This too was familiar, but I was ready for that trap as well. I wasn't about to become the sexual stimulant which turned them on to an evening of fucking without coming to terms with the basic questions. So I dove into the mix and laid out the reality that I saw. They dug its accuracy, and when I was finished Ina said, 'That's all true, but what do we do now?'

'Why, give me a massage, of course,' I said. The seeming irrelevancy of the answer was all the charm that was needed. 'All right,' she said. I looked at Michael. 'You too,' I said.

I lay down on the floor in front of the fire, face down, and let myself relax, not only my body, but all the strings I was pulling on the astral plane. Immediately I sank into the inner world, where all structures melt, and nothing is left but the movement of darkness and its flashes of light. Four hands touched me at once, Michael's strong, heavy fingers going to my spine, and Ina's delicate touch running up and down the backs of my legs. I felt simultaneously supported and tripped out. They began to work easily and methodically, touching and feeling different parts of me, and rubbing or caressing or stroking wherever it felt good for them to do so.

I floated a great distance from them, and their touch and voices came from afar. Ina's fingers began to stroke the insides of my thighs from the backs of my knees to my buttocks. Small electric charges pulsed up into my balls. Simultaneously, Michael pressed deep into my back with his thumbs, and I felt the spine crack, and the deep muscles protest and then relax. My breathing became full. I felt like a baby in the bath, with its parents washing it. I could feel the warmth flow through me from one to the other, and there was nothing for me to do but lie passive and feel the pleasure which coursed up and down my limbs and into my belly. Ina's hands moved to my ass and her fingers probed into the crack, prodding gently, forcing the muscles to let go. I found myself holding on, and to my surprise she spanked me lightly. 'Don't be afraid,' she said, and in a swoop brought her hand under my legs and cupped my cock and balls. 'He is so pretty, Michael, isn't he?' she crooned in that voice in which mothers cherish their children. Michael only grunted and grabbed my shoulders, pummeling them and drumming the tension out.

Deliciously, I felt her hands go around my waist and unbuckle my belt. The pants opened and she began to tug on them, drawing them toward my ankles. A cool breeze played over my bare legs and I trembled. 'Let's kidnap him, Michael,' she said, 'and lock him up here. Wouldn't it be nice to have a friend that we could keep for ever?' Part of me thrilled to her words and the intent behind them, while yet another part of me shuddered in fear. She suddenly seemed like a witch, casting some spell on my mind, and I was succumbing with ease and even gratitude. Michael's hands grabbed me roughly and spun me around so that I lay on my back. And then they took my shirt off.

I was totally naked, lying there with my eyes closed, and I could sense them kneeling near me, Ina at my feet, Michael at my head, and they were breathing heavily. A thousand fantasies rushed through my head and I dug all the potential in the moment. It was what it was and all the things it could be, simultaneously.

Ina's mouth put an end to all my speculations. First I felt her breath on my belly and, a long minute later, her tongue gently curving into my navel. My belly quivered. She drew back and leaned forward again, this time dropping her breasts to my chest. I started up, not having been aware that she'd removed her blouse and bra. She touched my skin with her nipples, very lightly, and then moved her torso back and forth so that the pendulous breasts traced intricate patterns on me. I drew my breath in sharply and heard her suck the air in through her lips. Michael leaned heavily onto my chest with his hands, and he grabbed the skin all around my nipples and started to pull and pinch, and kissed me as though he were a baker working with bread. I lost all ability to breathe and let his rhythm dictate the movement of my breath, as though I were receiving artificial respiration.

It was a rich sea of sensation that I dove into, and I let myself go to the sensual joy of the moment. And then something must have happened between them, because their hands now seemed to belong to one person. Ina ran her nails up and down my legs while Michael massaged my arms. They took the energy from the extremities and connected it in the torso. I felt myself alive in an extraordinary manner; I grew lighter, cleaner. I began to move from side to side as my body responded to the touch it was receiving, my mouth opened and my face lost all its tension. The more they rubbed me, the more I wanted to be covered. I wished there were dozens of people now, running their hands over my body, and licking me, and kissing me.

I began to move from side to side as my body responded to the touch it was receiving, my mouth opened and my face lost all its tension. The more they rubbed me, the more I wanted to be uncovered. I wished there were dozens of people now, running their hands over my body, and licking me, and kissing me.

And with that thought, I felt the hot wetness of Ina's mouth swoop down on my cock. I almost bent in half with the sensation. All of the energy that their massage had worked on had been herded into my belly and to the base of my cock, although I felt no specific sexual urge. But with her touch, all the sexual reality of the moment sprang immediately into view, and my cock hardened instantaneously. Michael stopped his movement and must have been watching her. I heard her moan and make slobbering sounds deep in her mouth, and felt her lips do their dance up and down the skin of my cock. Her tongue surpassed all in its delicacy and sensitively and lasciviousness. First she sucked, and then pulled back, and then did a job with her tongue, lapping up the length of the shaft in broad strokes, and moving down again, flicking the skin with just the very tip of her organ, until she reached the base of the rod and buried her mouth in my pubic hair, where she made little whimpering sounds and worked frantically down the patch of fur to the crack between my thighs and down into my balls, which she took in her mouth and licked from inside.

I wanted to move my pelvis and pump my cock into her, but I felt somewhat odd since there had been no formal transition from massage to sex, and Michael still loomed ominously over me. I wondered whether he would want me to suck him off, or fuck me. I was tentative and ready for anything, not sure what I was feeling except for the great furor at my cock.

Then Michael's voice cut through everything,

very calm and soft. 'Why don't you let him fuck you, Ina?' he said. At that I opened my eyes, just in time to see a look of crackling tension pass between them. Her lips curled and without warning she hurled herself at him, dropping her knee into my stomach. The wind went out of me and I rolled to one side, all the while watching the two of them. She went for his eyes with her nails and he knocked her arms to one side. 'I will kill you!' she shrieked.

I was torn between the drama of the fight and the way her breasts jiggled and how her ass whipped through the air. He was getting the worst of it because he wouldn't hit her, only ward off her blows. I couldn't read the subtleties of the situation: the throbbing in my cock was too distracting, so I followed my animal instincts and jumped her from behind. She was startled, and then started shouting and trying to punch at me. Michael grabbed her arms and I wrestled her to the floor. For a moment she lay there, panting and hateful, and I drank in the heaving of her breasts and the way her skirt had worked its way up her thighs, revealing her black-and-yellow-striped panties. I grabbed her legs and she kicked out at me. I pushed her back, and pinning her ankles under my thighs, I pulled at her skirt. She struggled so hard it was impossible to accomplish anything. 'We'll have to tie her,' I said. At that she screamed. 'And gag her,' he added.

I grabbed for my pants and pulled the belt off,

and then tied her ankles together. Michael turned her over, and with his belt secured her wrists together behind her back, and then wrapped his handkerchief around her mouth, muffling her sounds. She still tried to stop me, but this time it was fairly simple to slip the skirt down her legs and over her feet, leaving her in just her panties. I reached down and ripped the elastic band with my teeth, then slowly tore the garment right down the side until I could just lift it completely off her. She drew in her pelvis and tucked her cunt far back. But I had other plans. 'Where's the vaseline?' I asked. 'I'll get it,' Michael said, and went to fetch the jar.

I looked at her. 'I'm only doing this because I think it will help your marriage,' I said, and winked at her. She stared at me, and then a glint of humour came into her eyes. Michael returned with the jar. He looked very serious and competent, and seemed not at all excited. I rolled her over and put some of the jelly on my fingers. I parted her ass cheeks and lubricated the entire slot, right into her asshole. It was a bit tight, since her legs were tied together, but I enjoyed it that way. 'What am I doing?' asked Michael. 'You can stop it anytime you want,' I said. 'No,' he said, 'I need to see this.'

I rolled her over on her stomach and lowered myself onto her. My cock was now soft, and I hung my body above hers so that my limp tool would just touch the crack of her ass, and then I rocked back and forth, letting it trail up and down the entire length of the valley. At first she lay still, and then twitched her ass to reach for me. She said something into her gag and I reached down to untie it. 'You don't have to tie me any-more,' she said.

Michael took the two belts off and she stretched full out, her arms ahead of her and her legs spread wide apart. 'Go ahead,' she said, 'fuck me. Fuck me in the ass. I want you to.' As she talked my cock got hard and I slipped it down between her buttocks and neatly into the hole. She gasped and then relaxed, then raised her ass off the floor to take me in fully.

Oddly, I began to lose my excitement. My cock felt good and I could sense the heat and tightness of her asshole, the succulent potential of it. But I felt removed somehow, at a distance. And then I understood the reason. Michael was laying down very heavy vibrations of disapproval, although he was the one who had set it up. I looked over at him quizzically. He read my meaning and abruptly stood up and walked out of the room. A moment later we heard the front door slam.

And then the two of us began. There were a few seconds of awkwardness then, with the realisation that he was gone and we were doing him some kind of baroque favour. I drove my cock all the way up her ass. She arched her back and moaned mightily. I reached forward and cupped her bre-asts in my hands, pinching her nipples and massaging the full round globes. She tossed her head from side to side and let her mouth drop open. I brought up one hand and put two fingers into her mouth. She closed on them and began sucking greadily, lapping at them with her tongue. The double sensation of mouth and ass inflamed me and with my other hand I moved down to plunge my fingers into her cunt. She grunted and began to shake inside her body. I could feel the pressure on the top of her cunt, and when my fingers went all the way in, I touched my cock through the thin membrane separating the two openings. Her eyes bulged and she rocked her ass back and forth frantically, her mouth now drawing all the blood to the tips of my fingers.

I felt myself starting to come, so I stopped my motion, and forced her to hold still. I sat up on my haunches and had her lie down stretched out flat, her legs together, her arms at her sides. From the way I sat I could look straight down to her ass, and I pried the cheeks apart to expose my cock imbedded in the hole. I slid it in and out, watching the pink bud of her anus contract and expand to take in and let out the now steaming cock. I moved faster and faster, and began weaving from side to side, and then slamming in deeply, and coming out to tickle her asshole with the very tip of my cock. She groaned and raked at the rug with her nails, contracting her ass muscle so that it clutched at my cock like a large, strong, soft hand. She began sucking at my tool with her ass, dragging on it, pulling it in, trying to get the sperm to come rising out and shooting up. Again she began to succeed, and again I held back, this time slapping her ass to make her lie still. She relaxed and I brought my legs between hers, forcing her to spread her thighs apart, and then slowly slid my cock out of her ass.

She gasped and moved her ass around and toward me imploringly, all the while making little simpering noises with her mouth. I reached down and grabbed her snatch, catching the fur in my fingers and twisting it. She cried out and I pulled her cunt toward me, forcing her to raise her ass up and come to her knees. She lay there, her shoulders and face on the floor and the succulent delight of her ass and cunt waving before my eyes. I made four fingers into a single plane and inserted them directly into her hole. At first entry she flinched, and I stopped. I brought my face forward and began biting her ass with gentle teeth, not to hurt her but to loosen her up. I could feel her cunt letting go, and my hand slid in even further, up to the first knuckles, to the second knuckles, and the right up to the palm, and further. I pushed and she made choking sounds until my hand was in up to the joint of my thumb. For a long moment we froze like that, then I began to move my fingers inside her, scratching at her womb, rubbing it, twisting back and forth inside it. I drove my arms forward and her response was to move back and impale herself even further on my hand.

Then I crooked my thumb and inserted it into her asshole, so that now all five fingers were imbedded in her flesh. I made a pincer between my thumb and my other fingers and pulled it tight so that I held her by the membrane which joined asshole to cunt. With that leverage, I twisted and turned and made her stand and then squat. I grabbed her hair and pulled her head down, forcing her mouth to cover my cock once more. And I manipulated the movement of her tongue and lips by remote control as I varied the pleasure and pain levels at her crotch. She sucked on my hard cock, letting herself go into complete abandon. Her lips stretched wide as she slid up and down on the shaft of my cock, the saliva dribbling out from the corners of her mouth; then she was gulping to take the entire shaft in, into her throat, where she convulsed and gripped the head of my prick. Her hair flew wildly and her eyes were closed, and her ass moved in corkscrew gyrations as I pushed and pulled on the tender openings.

For the third time she brought me to the point of coming, and for the third time I stopped. I pulled her head off my cock and then rudely popped my fingers out of her holes. She gasped and lay there surprised, her legs akimbo, her breasts flat on her ribcage. I looked at the lush body and flung myself on her. Her face flushed with gratitude and her legs opened and went into the air to receive me. With no jockeying for position, I slid right into her waiting twat. And this time there was no stagecraft. I was hot and ready, and she sucked me in greedily. She pulled my ass into her and worked her hands in such a way as to get the rhythm she wanted out of me. I was glad to oblige. Her cunt worked like her mouth, tightening around my cock and then opening to let me lodge deeper inside her.

My lips found hers and we breathed into one another's mouths, our tongues massaging each other. It became all heat and motion, and the fantasy machine in my head was pouring out sheer pictures of reality, shots of me from behind as my ass contracted to thrust my cock into her and relaxed as I drew out, only to plunge again into the hot hole. Her breasts crushed my chest. Her ass curved, offering her cunt to me. Her arms pulling me into her, forcing me to jam my cock right to the wall of her womb, crashing against it brutally, until from inside me the sperm finally had its moment, and came churning and bubbling up to splash with a great wet burst into her box, when she let out a great sob and flung her pulsating pelvis into mine. Incredibly, we came fully and together, pumping our juices into each other, until there was nothing left and we subsided in one another's arms.

We lay that way for a long while, then disengaged. I pulled myself off her and looked down at her body. Her thighs glistened with sweat and my sperm, and her secretions oozed out of the bottom of her cunt. Her mouth was slack, her tongue peeking out to the corner of her lips. She looked as though she didn't want to move for a long while.

At that point, Michael came in. I wasn't sure whether he had been watching or not, but he was naked and had an erection. She saw him coming and seemed to want to pull herself away. Instead, she leaned subtly toward him. His face was set in a ruthless mask and his hands were clenched. She whimpered slightly as he knelt down next to her. He leaned forward and stuck his cock between her lips. She fought it but he knelt by her head and bought his full weight to bear. I got the impression that he had never been so overpowering before. Perhaps he needed to see his wife with another man, to remember that she was just a woman like any other woman, to be loved sometimes, and sometimes just to be used as a sexual object. The reason sex gets boring in marriage is that both partners forget how to be impersonal with one another.

But he was treating her like any slut right now. And she seemed to be torn between digging it and hating it. He moved down and planted himself between her legs. He pried them open and brought his large cock to the cunt lips. He regarded her for a long time, and then plunged in, hard and fast. She gasped and her legs shot up, involuntarily it seemed. He hooked his arms around the backs of her knees and forced her thighs to her chest, bringing her cunt all the way up and forward, totally exposed. And then he began slamming into her again and again, crashing into her ass and against her cunt. She cried out, 'No don't, Michael, don't do it,' But his fury gained in quantum leaps until his face was almost purple with rage, and he let go of her legs and starting hitting at her with his hands.

At first she tried to stop him, and then she became angry, and she began to punch back. In a moment they were rolling across the floor, still joined, slapping and hitting at each other, slamming their bodies into each other, scratching and kicking, spitting and yelling. Until they crashed into a large armchair and lodged there, Ina on her back jammed against the side of the chair, and Michael overwhelming her with his bulk and power. She gave up all her efforts to hit him and began sobbing. He became confused and pulled back, and the minute his cock left her, she rolled over on her side. He looked at her for a minute and then anger flashed again, and the realisation that he had somehow been tricked or cheated. He grabbed her body roughly, hoisted her on his lap, and began spanking her. She didn't move. His hand came down again and again, making the jiggling buttocks red and then violet, slapping her ass until she was all tears and supplications.

Then he pulled out from under her, put her torso up on the chair so that she knelt now, her ass poking back, and without ceremony brought his huge cock up and into her pussy. She received it silently and with great awareness. She pushed her ass back and engulfed his tool. He came up on his toes, his knees bent, so that he crouched over her like a dog, and thrust with all the power of his calf and thighs, his coiled legs driving him forward like a football player bucking into the opposing line. She was pinned and the chair was against the wall, so that she made an immovable cushion for him, a flesh dummy for him to pile into. As he did she didn't move or cry out, but seemed paralysed with ecstasy, letting him work his will on her without reserve, just being an open pussy for his cock, being a vessel for his wrath and sex and frustration, absorbing him.

I watched with interest and finally excitement. Cries began to form in his throat. The sweat glistened on his back. His face looked that of a wolf tearing at the flesh of a freshly killed deer. He grunted like a bear and his hands curved like talons and dug into her shoulders. The muscles on his legs bulged, and now he threw himself into her like a man hurling himself off a cliff. The wall shook and the chair shuddered and Ina seemed to sail into semi-consciousness as her small, tender cunt was ravaged. Finally a series of cries came from his throat, higher and fuller, until with, a loud long shout he shuddered up the entire length of him and bucked again and again into her, shooting what must have been a cupful of sperm into her elated cunt.

He slumped over her and in a moment slid to

the floor. She seemed plastered to the chair. I hoisted myself over the arm of the chair and sat down in it crosslegged, and raised her head to put it in my lap. Then holding her head up by the hair with one hand, I brought my cock to her mouth and inserted the tip of it between her lips. She did not move. Then, slowly and deliciously, I began pulling my cock, already very excited, until in a short time I felt the scalding geyser rise up until it spurted out. As the sperm came shooting out of my cock, I pushed her head forward so that I shot it deep into her throat. I kept my cock there until she swallowed, then pulled out.

We lay around like that for fifteen minutes, and then, one by one, we got up and stumbled off to different places, bathroom, bedrooms. I took a shower and put on some fresh clothes, and noted that it was only nine o'clock and I wasn't sleepy. I went downstairs to find Ina making coffee and Michael putting some music on the stereo. They were both dressed and seemed very calm. If anyone had come in just then they would have found a very mundane scene, a suburban psychiatrist and his lovely wife entertaining a friend for an overnight stay. The three of us looked at one another, and it became immediately clear that no one wanted to talk about what had happened. It was rich and complex, and each of us undoubtedly had a hundred possible ways of looking at it. But we all felt quite delicious and cool, and any post mortem psychologising would have taken the fine edge off the mood.

There was no way of knowing what this would do for their marriage, or our friendship, but I suspected that no drastic changes would take place. And whether we did something like this again would depend entirely on circumstance and mood. I looked at Ina; she smiled inside herself at me, and looked away. I looked at Michael; he winked and smiled. I thought of Regina. If she were here, the four of us could . . .

And then I tripped over myself. No matter how I turned and moved, no matter where I went, every time I turned an important corner, there was Regina. It seemed as though there were some great finger in the sky pointing at her, trying to make me understand something in relation to her. At the moment I felt no need for her, nor any romantic love for her; but her presence was thorough and implacable. And as I walked into the kitchen, I resolved that I would have to plumb the situation more deeply yet. It seemed that Regina was destined to be a part of my life no matter what my conscious mind decided. Socially I might want to be alone, but zoologically, I needed a mate. And no matter how I tried to get around it, the mate seemed to be her. The thought simultaneously gladdened and depressed me, as Ina came in with a tray of refreshments.

(8)

YES, THIS WAS the way it should be. The woman's body beneath me, her eyes closed as her face showed a kaleidoscope of emotions, biting her lips, opening her mouth in breathy wonder. Diana opened her legs even further, and her legs and pelvis became a tree trunk and ocean, the thick thighs spread out and leading into her hips, the whole area a wide fleshy pool of sensation. And then her narrow waist rising out of it, curving gracefully up to her boyish torso which then exploded in ripe, sensitive breasts. Her arms lay above her head, as though she were tied to a post, and they too made a long sweeping line from her wrists to her armpits, which now showed in all their hairy vulnerability. I was raised up on my knees and hands, my arms stiffly supporting my body. And my cock lay imbedded in her cunt. From where I looked, I could see the gleaming shaft rising and falling from her pubic hair.

My cock was like a lever and all the buttons were inside her pussy. If I moved up, she would twitch and roll her ass. If I moved to the side she would bring one leg up. If I dropped down and sank deep into her from below, bringing my cock directly between her legs and vertically up into her hole, she shuddered and gasped and brought her hands up to grab my shoulders. She was like a sensual puppet, inert and ready to respond to every manipulation. I admired her great ability to be passive, to trust to her own feelings and the fact that I wouldn't hurt her. So many women kept constantly on guard, waiting for something to go wrong, waiting for the pleasure to depart, that they never were able to just let go and let it happen to them.

I reached down and nipped Diana on the breast. Her eyes opened in surprise and then she smiled. She brought my head down and raised up to place her lips on mine. Her mouth was all giving. It was as though she were speaking a fluid and alien language, very rapidly and in total silence. And although I didn't understand any of the words, the meaning was totally clear. Her tongue became a wonder worker, licking my face, teasing my lips.

I slid my hands along her arms and pinned her wrists to the couch. She let herself fall back again and gave herself to the experience. I leaned down and licked all the skin from between her breasts to her throat, and then around to her jaw and up to her ear. When I plunged my tongue deep inside her ear, she moaned loudly and began grinding her pelvis against me. Her cunt became a hot wet hand squeezing my cock, grabbing it insistently, loving it with a singular intensity. I felt myself sinking into the sloshing tightness of her box when her legs came up and wrapped themselves around my waist. I breathed hotly into her ear and lapped at all the delicate bony ridges inside and around the edge. I felt her nails dig into my forearm. 'Talk to me,' she said, 'tell me what you want.'

I was caught short by the request, and then I let the fantasies go. 'I want your open cunt a million miles wide. You're all pussy, baby, all the way up to your eyes. Nothing but cunt and ass, big ass. I want you to go down and lick my cock, and just keep sucking it and loving it until you can't keep your mouth open anymore.' As I spoke, her breath became heavy and she began to move faster, more rhythmically, now pumping her cunt against me harder. 'I want to spread you over a bed, with your beautiful cunt flying high and your ass inviting, and then have a hundred men come in to see you, to watch you pull your cheeks open, and beg them to fuck you.' She began to moan and writhe. 'You want it too, don't you, you little bitch,' I whispered. 'You want to have all those cocks in your mouth, to have them all come on your tongue so you can swallow them all. You want to go begging on your knees to have them fuck you in the ass. I want to take you in the ass, right now.' She keened and pulled me closer with her legs. 'No,' she said, 'please, not now, just keep fucking me.'

'You want me to fuck you?' I said. 'Yes, please.' I pulled my cock back and kept it at the tip of her cunt. She strained up for it, to bring it into her cunt. 'Beg,' I said. 'Tell me what you're willing to do.'

'I'll do anything,' she sobbed.

I pulled out of her completely and immediately moved up to her face. She looked at me and a shadow of fear passed through her eyes. I brought my cock up to her mouth, and then leaned down. 'Start licking,' I said. She made a small shrugging motion with her shoulders and her tongue came out to begin its tiny path up the length of my cock. I brought my balls up and dropped them on her mouth. Her tongue kept working, kept moving. Finally I covered her face entirely and felt her mouth go for the sensitive strip between balls and asshole, and she hungrily sucked at it, and ran her tongue up and down in thick, wet strokes. I reached down and pinched both her nipples. Her knees came up and she grabbed my thighs, to force my body to sink more heavily onto her mouth.

I moved back and brought my cock into play, rubbing it all over her face, and on her lips, and then she opened her mouth and with a despairing sigh let the rod sink deep into her. I knelt by her head so that she had to turn her face sideways to suck me off, and then I told her to bring herself off. She stopped sucking and her eyes opened to seek mine. There was a begging request to not do it. 'Do it,' I said.

Then, gently, tentatively, her right hand moved down her body until it rested on her crotch. 'Do it.' I said again. Her legs opened slowly and her hand moved down between her thighs. Her middle finger curved down and slid into her wet cunt all the way up to the knuckle, and then came out again. 'Come on,' I said, 'pretend you're alone. I want to watch.' I pulled my cock out of her mouth and sat back. She closed her eyes and brought the tip of her finger to her clitoris. She started to stroke it lightly, up and down, and suddenly her entire body changed. It became wired, electrified. Her knees came up and her nipples became hard with ridges running through them. She began to roll her head from side to side and her ass started a small pumping motion.

Then the tip of her finger started moving like a vibrator, shaking her clitoris, jiggling it, flicking at it. She started to moan and thrash about. I moved down and lay between her legs. Her cunt was now running juices and very inflamed. I brought my mouth right up to it and drank in the heady aroma. It was too much at once, and with a groan I plunged into her churning pussy. My tongue sank into that steamy box and began lapping at the honey which flowed from it. Her other hand came down and inserted itself into her cunt. I licked and nipped at her cunt lips, and then brought my tongue up to her clitoris, lapping at it and at her finger. Finally, she took her hand away and used both her hands to spread her cunt lips apart, prying them open like a nutshell. The pink slimy inner lips were exposed, and I could feel the tight granular opening, the tiny bud which gave access to the inner heat. She pulled so hard that I thought she would rip her cunt apart.

Now it was pure feasting. I ran my tongue like a scoop from the deep crack of her ass up past her pulsating asshole, between her thighs, and up the length of her dripping pussy, to end right on her clitoris which I took and bit gently with my teeth. Dozens of times I made the same trip, until I had found the rhythm that turned her on. Now I was her sexual object, letting myself have no other function than to give her pleasure, and doing that by finding what gave me the most pleasure. Sensitive to myself, I was best for her. The sweep of my tongue up her privates became richer each time, for now my tongue paused momentarily to dig at her asshole, and changed speed and width between her legs, and plunged deeply into her cunt as I swept between the lips. Her cunt now became a bellows, swelling with air as it bellied in, and then letting the air out with a wet rush.

Finally she began to come. It started in her legs with a deep trembling. Her moans got deeper and rougher. Her fingers twined themselves in my hair and pulled at my scalp, sending tingles up and down my spine. Her ass was like a forest fire, crackling and jumping with awesome speed and strength. My mouth became as excited as my prick, and I lost all sense of what I was doing. I became a slobbering, moaning slave, licking at her cunt, sucking and lapping and moaning into her opening, begging for her to come, begging her to spend all the deepest musky fluids, and discharge them as the waves of energy rolled through her body. And then, with an unearthly cry, she threw her legs high into the air, and her cunt convulsed totally into my mouth, lips quivering, vagina vibrating, the cunt hole itself opening and closing in rapid spasms, and then the juice gushing out, as I drove deep into her and sucked every last drop out, until she was absolutely dry.

Her legs came down slowly and rested on my shoulders. I lay there for a few minutes and then extricated myself. I sat up abruptly and went off into the kitchen. I felt disappointed and a little disgusted with myself. I felt as though I had just seen the same movie for the hundredth time. It was a good movie and I enjoyed it each time, but it seemed fatuous to keep seeing it.

Regina had called me that morning, angry and hurt. She wanted to be in my life, she said, and she was willing to come to New York. She was capitulating rapidly, ready to give up many things just to be with me. And she was still being faithful to me; that's how she wanted it. Once she told me that, when an affair had ended with someone with whom she had been very much in love (although, as she said, 'I didn't know him as well as I know you,') she didn't fuck for months afterwards. It was a clue to her temperament: the romantic bitch. And now it was the same scene, the combination of 'I am strong enough for you,' and 'I can't live without you.' And as usual, I fell for it, letting her do her bitch act, to be followed by her baby voice. And by the time she had hung up I had promised to fly out to the Coast in mid-May, to drive back here with her and her kid for the summer. And then we would make plans for the fall in the fall.

The moment I hung up, I felt as though I had been had. She wouldn't take 'no' for an answer, and I was her accomplice, or at least some aspect of me was. I spent a good part of the day sulking and running down vicious dialogues in my head, and after dinner, I 'found myself' in Diana's neighbourhood. So I dropped over. She was alone, and after a bit of chitchat we went right to fucking. We have known each other over a year, were once fierce lovers, a Scorpio-Leo confrontation, split up, and have become fucking buddies since. There's a line that describes it: 'ex-lovers like cracked china meet.'

To say that I fucked Diana to spite Regina is perhaps an accurate oversimplification. At the moment I felt shitty because it seemed I had used Diana as a prop in my inner drama. I put on water for coffee and Diana came in, very solicitous. She put her head on my shoulder.

'Something's wrong,' she said.

'Yeah,' I answered.

'I can always tell. Whenever you don't fuck me after eating me, I know it's not all right with you.'

I smiled and kissed her. 'You are a marvellous practical woman,' I said. 'Too bad you're a Leo.'

'Who is she?'

'Her name is Regina. And she lives in California. And she's pretty bad in bed, and a bitch to boot, and dependent at the drop of a hat, and very ballsy, and tricky and unscrupulous. And really a decent chick but not anyone I want to get all excited about. And somehow she's got her hooks into my soul and I can't shake her loose.'

'That doesn't sound right,' she said. 'I've never known a woman to hold you when you didn't want to be held on to. There's something in you that wants her.'

'It may sound stupid,' I said, 'but I think I love her. And it's all wrong. I mean, it's not what I would have wanted, and I don't even have the feeling that goes with it.'

Diana continued the conversation by bringing her hand down to my cock and fondling it gently. I felt my rod stirring. 'I don't feel right about this,

Diana,' I said. But she silenced me in the best way possible, by dripping to her knees and putting her mouth around my dick. Suddenly all thoughts of Regina became two-dimensional. I mean, they still ran through my mind, but they had lost all power to affect me. It was like meditation, where I can sit and watch the thought machine produce its effects and not get involved in any of its products to the exclusion of a total awareness of reality. I wondered what the Theosophical Society would do with the proposition that a good blow job was easily the equal of sitting quietly in the full lotus. I wondered whether Madame Blavatksy was a virgin and whether it was true that Gurdjieff liked little boys.

I looked down at the goddess licking my cock. She was kneeling in the lion pose and tonguing my balls from underneath, moving her lips up the shaft and gobbling the head, then, with a deep breath, bringing her head all the way forward and lodging my cock deep in her throat. Her ass stuck out behind and her breasts jiggled as she worked. I flashed for a moment that it would be a groove to have another man there fucking her in the ass while she ate me, and for perhaps the thousandth time I regretted that I only had one body, and only one cock. I leaned over and ran my hands down her back, letting my nails raise tiny red trails along the spine. She shuddered with delight and grabbed my cock in her hands, pulling it now, jerking off into her own mouth. I felt a kind of disinterested excitement. All the usual sensations coursed through me, but I experienced them as from a distance. I felt extremely cosmic, viewing the known universe from its periphery, watching the galaxies dance, and the many manifestations of energy do their thing. In the incredible far-away was our own scene, a speck of rock chugging around a middle-sized, middle-aged sun in a medium-sized cluster of stars. And among the smallest specks on the speck was poor old Diana kneeling on the kitchen floor sucking my cock for all she was worth, and me digging it, half out of a sense of responsibility and half out of spontaneous enjoyment.

I reached over and grabbed her under the arm-pits and brought her to her feet. Her eyes were dazed and her mouth a slur of flesh, wet and obscene. She looked like every drugged cock-sucker in every piece of pornography that had ever appeared. Of course she was beautiful. It is only our prejudice, our insistence on prim trim-ness of visage, which makes the dripping cunt-face seem disgusting, when in fact a woman is never more breathtaking than at that moment when every aspect of her essential animal is shown, with heaving breasts, hair stringy around her shoulders, excited ass and hungry twat. This was Diana now, a nameless lusting mouth, want-ing cock, wanting the slobbering penetration, wanting gobs of sperm on her tongue, wanting to be pushed down and opened, to be overwhelmed

177

and elevated all at the same time. Mother and child and witch and virgin all at once, the Cocksucker Deity, Queen of All Cunt.

I turned her around and had her bend over the kitchen table. Her knees shook as she bent to let her torso lie flat on the wooden surface. Her cunt gaped at me and the cheeks of her ass spread wide. Between them the tiny hairs were wet and sticky, and formed a web with globules shining, reflecting the overhead light. Still cool, still balanced, I laid my cock into her. She groaned out loud. 'Oh God,' she said. 'Please do it. Fuck me good. Fuck me the way I like it. Fuck me the way you know how.'

'Keep your head, Diana,' I said. 'Stay awake.'

'If I go under,' she said, 'come get me.'

'Right,' I said, as I began to fuck her. And it was just that. It wasn't us fucking, it was me doing it to her, doing it in her, doing it for her. She had to do nothing but lie there, letting her cunt be open. And I began to dance. It was the total dance, the dance of Shiva, the cosmic movement which sustains all movement. I went through all the animal and spirit forms, became everything from a dog to a demon. I growled and hissed, sang and prayed, words poured out like sap from a tree. And everything I was I poured on her, sank into her.

She was silent, but it was a silence that spoke of immense feeling, of deep concentration. Her whole life was in her cunt, while her mind remained alert, aware of the kitchen, of the city, of time, of space, of eternity. She was taking the male role in the Tantric act, while I played the female, and the fact that she had the cunt and I the cock made no difference. Her cunt grew rank with pleasure and meaning. I touched every inch of it, every crevice got penetrated, every wrinkle was straightened. I was every man who had ever fucked any woman, who ever could. Her ass rose higher, the globes gleaming like dew-covered crystal. Her asshole opened and a thin stream of gas escaped. Her cunt bubbled over. I moved inside her for what seemed an endless time. There was nothing to stop me, nothing to make her want me to stop. We were home, where we wanted and needed to be, where each of us in this poor bedraggled species wants to be living, but instead we march around like silly suited zombies and exchange money, and shuffle papers, and make wars.

But fucking is God, fucking is how it begins, fucking is what it is all about while we are here. In fucking everything is contained, all the opposites meet, and there is anger and humour, love and hate, aggression and tenderness. Fucking is where consciousness begins, in that fatal separation of the sexes. In fucking we are whole once more, and out of that wholeness (oh, divine ironic paradox!) another child is born, another fragment, another splinter who will in his or her turn strive to be completed. The history of the world spun from our cock and cunt, and everything that was within the power of the mind to know, we knew then, all mathematics all ethics all poetry all feeling all thought all sensation all the ages of man and all the changes of woman. And then, when we had soared to the outermost reaches of knowledge, we burst through that thin skin and dove into the unknown, the mysterious, the *that* for which there is no concept, no symbol . . . the simple blinding awareness of Being.

And in that state, at that timeless moment, I heard a great cry rising up, and a tremendous shout as if it were a huge choir of praising voices or a field of bodies in torment, and the me who was the animal fucking the Diana who was the animal, was leaping in great spastic jumps, my cock tearing and ramming into her gashlike hole, while she wailed at the top of her lungs, and bucking like goats, we came and came, pumping our juices and heat and yearning and understanding into one another, into the void which joined us, until a great joyful peace rose up our legs and into our groins and through our chests and arms and heads, and we sank slowly to the floor.

We lay there for five minutes, and the only sound was our breathing and the water boiling on the stove. Finally Diana took a deep breath and said, 'You sure can fuck.' I smiled. 'Too bad it's for such a limited audience; just you, me, and God.'

'The only trouble with it,' she said, putting her

head on my chest, 'is that it's so overwhelming, so impersonal, so fucking cosmic, that I can't even relish it afterwards. It's like sunrise in the Grand Canyon.'

I looked at her. 'My God, another romantic. You want memories yet.'

'I suppose I'm still a bit old-fashioned,' she said. 'I'd like my ego to participate a bit more. Just my luck to get caught up in an Oriental Renaissance.'

'Let's have some coffee,' I said.

'That's very Zen,' she said, kissing me and getting to her feet.

We had coffee and I stayed the night. She had things to do, some sewing and other affairs, so I amused myself by getting stoned on some old hash she had lying around and watching Johnnie Carson in colour with the sound off. I hallucinated that he was the most enlightened man of our time, being able as he was to control the minds of fifty million people each night. I watched him do his mime, never stopping, never letting his attention waver, always in command. And once, when his eyes swept from right to left, as his gaze passed the television camera, I peered right into his soul, and saw fierce fires of intelligence. I couldn't tell whether I was projecting, going mad, or discovering a truth which would shock America. I called Diana over and told her about it, but she just patted my head and said, 'I think that hash was a little mouldy. Maybe you shouldn't smoke any more of it.'

I sank blissfully into my chair, thinking how nice it was to have a level-headed woman around, and the thought occurred to me that I could make it with Diana very easily, and have the entire pie, great sex and humour, and cosmic perspective, and no hassle about moving to California. I looked at her over my shoulder, and in an instant I realised that if I were to enter that special relationship called 'bonded' or 'mated' or 'married' with her, then all the joy and lightness and real respect for each other's identity would fly right out the window.

No, solving the problem went deeper than who I was with. The problems I faced with Regina were as much universal as specific, and it was with my own indecision that I had to come to terms. I felt somehow that I was near to some understanding which would cast things in an entirely new light, that in a stroke I would know why I clung to Regina as a symbol, and how I would extricate myself from the pattern of clinging and rejection which marked my so-called serious relations with women.

I sank back in my chair and again watched Johnnie Carson, who now looked a lot like Howdie Doodie, do his number on the heads of the population. I tried to look into tomorrow, but it was all trackless desert. And while I had enough food and water to sustain me, I had no direction at all.

(9)

THE NEXT DAY, Carol walked into my life.

To say I was swept off my feet would be to undervalue my experience. She grabbed me up like a whirlwind, and swept me into a strange land which had all the uncanny familiarity of a dream bordering on nightmare. She was young, only twenty-one, with red hair, and a body like a ripe pear. The usual adjectives don't do her justice for it wasn't in any particular physical characteristic that she shone, but with a sense of presence, a kind of openness and readiness for life that radiated from her.

She was one of that new generation of women who have been raised on probabilities of atomic annihilation and a great deal of dope. Among other things she was extremely brilliant, not in any bookish fashion, but with a razor-sharp mind that cut immediately through any artifice. Her lack of culture made her at once devastating and boring, for her insights were as superficially understood by her as they were potent in their suggestion to me. Her parents had been imprisoned in a concentration camp in Germany, had miraculously escaped with their lives, and were now settled in a mild haze of constant anxiety on a chicken farm in Jersey. She was raised in an atmosphere of retroactive fear, and the quickness of her lifestyle was due in large part to her unconscious need to keep moving, to escape whatever nameless dread her parents had inculcated in her when she was a child.

She had been on the road since she was sixteen, living with a wide range of men, including a rising figure in English politics. They had met in England and he set her up as his mistress in a Portuguese villa. Sporadically she had attended college, snaking in and out of the academic scene with ridiculous ease, using her cunt where her wile failed. Her entire orientation was to the moment, and any relationship, any situation, was merely another stop along the route. She had no sense of destination, merely an air of travel. Without being self-conscious about it, she ran a cosmic trip.

Of course, the other aspects of her personality were suppressed. The frightened little girl, the self-destructive woman, the bitch, the mother . . .

none of these showed as she put on her act for the world. She covered all her uncertainty with bravado.

She was staying at a friend's house, and was in a strange condition. She had been crashing frantically for months, and no one, not even her oldest friends, could put up with her for more than a week. She was so theatrical, so bent on making an effect without any consideration for other realities, that ultimately she became tedious. I had gone up to visit Ray, and found Jan, a faded forty-year-old who just wanted to sleep for a long, long time, and Carol, who immediately charmed me out of my privacy. Within an hour our rap had become so heady that I invited her to come stay with me for a week or so. All the warning bells in the back of my head were muffled by the excitement I felt at the thought of all that energy and intelligence in bed, and what would be uncovered with the mask dropped away and the woman came forth.

It is a beautiful thing about women, that no matter how ugly or shallow they are in their social lives, the minute they begin to be fucked really well, they become deep, sensual, moaning animals, capable of great subtlety and passion, able to enter into deep communication and even communion on profound levels of their being. And with a woman like Carol, I foresaw a great revelation.

On the way to my place she began some of her

usual tricks. At one point she hit a cop on the back with her walking stick, and he, with the doltishness of the insecure male who feels he is being mocked, turned all of his malevolence on me. I smiled my way out of the scene and we continued downtown. On the subway she was outrageous, mixing honest good humour and friendliness with a coy attempt at flair, so that more than half of her routine failed. I had no other interest than to get safely to my pad, where an evening of dope and sex waited.

We finally arrived, and immediately there was a huge awkwardness between us. The audience had disappeared, and we were like the players in *Rosencrantz and Guildenstern* who suddenly find themselves playing a murder in the desert with the watchers gone. At once we were stripped of roles, and cast about to find some identity. We knew one another not at all, and both of us were too intelligent to pretend that what was happening wasn't really happening. So a weird thing happened. We began playing to each other.

She went into a kind of falsetto voice and I assumed a gruff pose. We went through the paces of smoking dope and putting on some music. This was a scene I had done scores of times, as had she. The pick-up, the excitement, the desire for sex, and the awful gap between wanting and doing. We played with the ironic edge of the situation, pretending we were flirting so that we could flirt, pretending that we were growing close so that we could grow close. As the dope hit my brain and I began to spin off into fantasy-reality, I flashed that in a while we might be pretending we were fucking so that we really could fuck.

I was being warped by my own theory. For years I had preached metatheatre, the way of approaching life as a drama. And now it was all coming home, in the eyes of a mocking, bitter-sweet, heartbreaking, and lustful young stranger, who taunted me to be strong enough to sustain the tragedy of our condition. Part of me wanted to rip away the veil of staged distance, and simply let myself be exposed to her, with all my fears and insecurities and ambivalence. I wanted her to see me, to hold me, to let me be the totality of who I am. And yet I was locked in the role, and had to follow it through, putting on a cynicism that I honestly didn't feel.

In a flash I saw myself stripped naked, all the games I play hanging out. It was a beautiful moment, but there was no one to share it with, for Carol stood there behind her own mask, unwilling to let herself be full. So, like mannequins, we played our roles, did our grotesque hip minuet around one another's consciousness.

The time arrived, and no matter how close to the edge we pushed the drama, there was no way for an easy transition. So I stood up and said, 'Let's go to the bedroom.' She rolled her eyes in mock astonishment and said, 'Ohhh, I'll bet he wants to fuck me.' Part of me enjoyed the bravura of her style, and part of me cried out silently in disgust and loneliness. But only lust prevailed, and with great grimaces and mock bows, we escorted one another to the bed, took off our clothes, and lay down.

Immediately the mood changed. She became, all at once, mundane. Seemingly from nowhere, she began a chatter of inanities, a litany of names and experiences, recounting all her old lovers and casual fucks. She confessed that she might be pregnant, that she had gone to a bar a month ago and there met a sullen black cat to whom she confessed her loneliness and horniness. She asked him to accompany her to the loft where she lived with her current boyfriend, who wasn't home at the time. Of course, the man took her up three flights of stairs, and then grabbed her. She tried to talk him out of raping her, but almost simultaneously began taking off her bell-bottoms.

He bent her over the railing, exposing her luscious ass to his greedy eyes. How many times has this scene been enacted? Leroi Jones has penned it to perfection with his line about 'bagel babies and A-trainers.' The bored and animal black cat, and the nervous tittering white chick, acting out the penance they have to pay for three hundred years of slavery. He rammed his cock into her pussy, and fucked her violently. What feelings coursed through her, as with her conscious mind she put down the scene, and yet with all her neurotic need sucked the prick deep into her, expiating some hidden sin?

'He got pissed off,' she said, 'because I wasn't moving enough. But I didn't want to give him *everything*.'

'And you got pregnant,' I said, my voice cold and my heart beating. I hadn't even fucked her yet, and already I was jealous. Part of me thrilled at the sluttishness of her, and I realised in an instant that she was a total whore. I knew I could get her to do anything, to play any kind of perverse game, and make her like it. I could go down the entire route, shoving broomsticks up her, and grinding her face into the floor with my feet. I could use her like some scummy rag, and then, when I was finished, discard her, and have her beg and promise even greater debaucheries to allow her to come back. But at the same time I saw the fragility of her, the crying need, the broken person underneath the brazen chick. And as I looked down at the nakedness of her lush breasts, so young and vulnerable, and put my hand tremblingly on her nipples, I almost cried at the pain in her and in myself, and at the awful condition of mankind, that we should find ourselves in such stupidity and alienation.

I listened to her prattle for over an hour, being alternately bored and horrified, titillated and repulsed. Finally I could take no more, and I just moved forward brusquely to cover her mouth with mine. Instantaneously, she changed. All the warmth and richness of her came to the fore. With a small moan, she put her tongue into my mouth, and threw her arms around my neck. Now she was little girl, needing to be held, needing comfort. And I gave that to her, holding her very tightly, crushing my chest against her breasts, squeezing the hurt out of her, and giving her the solidity of my presence. We lay a long time in one another's arms, letting each other be a poultice for our shared pain. I flashed that we were like two walking open wounds, vulnerable to all the shit in life, and yet ready to soar into great depths of realisation and meaning.

I put my hand down between her legs and felt the fine pubic hair. Her cunt was surprisingly small, and not very wet. The mood switched from solace to sexuality. I pulled back and looked down at her. Her eyes were unfocused and swimming, her mouth open and wet. I leaned down and put my mouth on one of her breasts, gently licking the taut flesh, biting the nipple between my teeth. She groaned and rocked her pelvis back and forth. I inserted one finger into her cunt, and felt the inner walls give way. She massaged my finger with her box, and I felt the great rolling of the inner lips and the deep passage leading to the vacuum of her vagina. For a moment I sank into the wonder of the sensation and the beauty of the woman, but then I immediately remembered that she could be this way with any man, that her reactions were reflexes, that her fucking was stereotypic. And lust and heartbreak arose side by side. I wanted desperately to love her, and all I could do was fuck her. And what else could she accept right now? 'Love is not enough,' said Bettelheim, and I knew what he meant. The kind of deprivation she knew could not be filled by any man giving her his all. She would have to painfully retrace her life to its roots and rework all the traumas through. That would be hard work, and required a great degree of seriousness; but she was merely giddy.

I let my other hand roam over her, feeling the lush fullness of her breasts, letting her suck at my fingers with her mouth, and all the while inserting my other hand deeper into her, provoking the heat and juice that welled up in her cunt. Then the thoughts abruptly ended, and we were all over one another. I let all other considerations vanish as I sank into her. Impulse sent me scurrying down her body, and I buried my face between her legs. The rich aroma of her pussy assailed my nostrils, and I burrowed deep to taste the juices that edged around her cunt lips. She was luscious, fleshy and sticky. I probed her with my hand and licked her with my tongue. Her ass squirmed on the bed, and she cried out again and again, unintelligible sounds and moans.

She groped for me and I turned my body around so that my cock was at her mouth. She took it inside her at once, and the warm wet of her lips covered the tender head. She licked gently and with great awareness. Then we rolled over, and I was on top of her, grabbing her ass with both hands, and kissing and lapping at her cunt with a wild frenzy, while I ground my pelvis into her face. She took my cock deep in her throat and gagged on it. I pulled out and she kissed it with her lips as it slithered from her mouth, and then she pulled my ass down again, so that my cock plunged once more into her throat.

The trouble with sixty-nine is that what is being done to one distracts from what one is doing, and vice versa. We didn't know each other well enough to be able to do a complete dance, so we alternated, my eating her and her sucking me, until that entire energy had been expended. And then it was time to fuck.

Entering a woman for the first time is always an adventure. Each cunt is different, even though all cunts are the same. I turned around again and ranged my body over her. She looked up at me with intelligent longing, conscious of her role, conscious of our strangeness. There was absolute communication between us. Soul spoke to soul. And I loved her at once, as she did me. There was no time to think, or to ponder why such a thing was impossible and couldn't work. There was only the moment, and I knew that I had found my mate. In a flash, all the hesitancies and rationalisations I had about Regina disappeared, and I knew why I had suffered so much ambivalence. Despite all the seeming feelings to the contrary, I didn't love her, not like this, not with this total letting-go and ecstasy.

With our eyes locked, with our bodies poised, I slowly entered her, and oh! what a joining that was! Physical perfection in an instant, a cunt that snugly grabbed my cock and held it lovingly, a warmth that penetrated throughout my entire groin, a sweetness that drenched my body and which I could taste in my mouth. With a sigh we melted into one another.

The rest was all dance. Her ass moving in slow undulations, her breasts two mounds of softness nestling into my chest, her hands a loving caress up and down my spine. I could not feel or touch or taste her enough all at once. All the hunger that had been in me, all the need that I hadn't even been aware of, bubbled up and demanded to be fed. And with great gulping thrusts I brought my cock like a snout into the trough of her cunt, there to gorge myself on the entirety of it, the beauty and mystery, the ugliness and betrayal. In a stroke I wiped out all the men she had known, and she drained from me the memory and desire for all women.

Our heads were in perfect tune. There were no thoughts in our minds, simply the flow of abstract patterns of energy shuttling between us and forming a coherent tapestry of our consciousness. Our bodies blended and joined. And then, with a cry, I experienced what I had not known since I was nineteen, when for the first, and almost last, time I fucked a woman with whom I had no reservations, whom I trusted totally, and who later betrayed me. I felt my heart burst, and wave after wave of sadness and joy flowed from my deepest part and bathed her and buoyed us up.

In a stroke I saw the shallowness and childishness of all the fucking I had ever done, how I had played the games of cosmic consciousness and pretended to be a debauchee. This was different in its reality. It was people, it was on the planet Earth, it was dirt and sweat, it was mortality and limitation. And it was glorious.

Her legs went up slowly and languorously. Like two supple arms they embraced my waist, and her cunt opened like some mammoth cave. Deep deep and deep, black and violent and soft, tender and eternal and home. I cried out her name again and again, pouring all I had into myself and into her, and she received and reverberated. We became the amplification of one another. And from a great distance, yet from very close, a long sighing slide began, down a great snow slope, fast and powdery, clean and light, and we sank plunging down the incline to a great edge, where in each other's arms we hurtled free into space.

At the summit of our glide, I was suddenly and immediately in her arms, on my bed, with all the fears and suspicions, the memories and inhibitions, the realisation that she was a stranger to me, and with a full breath I swallowed the totality of the moment and felt the scalding heat coursing through my veins, my limbs trembling. I was totally free of all control, and the energy which coursed through me was the total life force which lay bottled in my tenseness. Now it was flapping and flying, and as I let myself go, she began to cry, a great yearning 'yes' which filled my ears and thundered through the room. It rose in volume and intensity until it sounded like the primeval OM. And in a sustained burst, I let loose the full load of sperm churning up from inside me, into her incredible cunt, which like a sensitive and conscious mouth, kissed and held and sucked all the fluid from my cock, and swallowed it deep into her vagina and even symbolically into her womb.

We clung to each other for a long, long time, and then slid into a peaceful oneness, male and female undifferentiated, simple humanity breathing and throbbing in a delicious afterglow. Slowly we parted, and I rolled to her side. And after a few minutes I opened my eyes to look at her. I couldn't believe her vast beauty, the sheer thereness of her. And at an instant, Regina died inside me.

(10)

CAROL STAYED WITH me for two weeks. It was the most hectic, confused, and glorious period of time I have ever spent with a woman. Her madness increased in proportion to the degree she trusted me. And I lost all perspective on what we were doing with one another. In the evening she would walk past where I was sitting, her ass a provocative outline against her jeans, her breasts hanging inside a shirt always opened at the front, and no matter what I was doing, I would reach for her. At times she was mocking, laughing at me all the while she pulled me in; and again, she could be unbelievably hot, suddenly falling into my lap and rubbing my face with her breasts, grabbing my cock with her hands and massaging it until I squirmed with pleasure.

We must have fucked about three times a day. I had no sense of time or duration. All the switches were open and both engineers were asleep at the throttle. The train was plummeting at high speed straight ahead, and neither of us cared about destination or result. This was something that I had been starved for. A woman who, despite all her hangups and weirdness, was totally open and gave of herself without hassle and without strings attached.

During that time I let all my affairs go, not doing any writing, nor seeing too many friends. Once Regina called and she sounded like a total stranger. She began talking about the house we would live in and the glorious weather on the Coast, and it sounded like a dreary article from a gardening magazine. I remembered now, all the fights, all the spitefulness, all the meanness of our relationship, and whatever had been good about it faded from view. I was extremely cold and curt and told her I didn't feel like talking, that I would call her back. To my surprise, she simply acquiesced, taking my words at face value. Ordinarily she would have whined about the shortness of the conversation, and tried to interest me in another round of talk. My antenna quivered. 'Is anybody there?' I said. 'Only Michael,' she answered. 'Who's Michael?' I wanted to know. 'Oh, he lives a few houses down. We were just sitting around getting stoned, and we were going to do some nude sunbathing in the back when you called.'

Hot lava ran down my chest. I couldn't believe my ears, nor could I accept my own reaction. Just seconds earlier I was rollicking with Carol, all thoughts of Regina relegated to the distant past. And I was ready to dismiss Regina on the phone without a spark of warmth. And now, suddenly, I was seething with jealousy. I saw the two of them lying in the grass, the hot sun baking their bodies, sweat forming pools in her navel. I could feel the heaviness of the air, hear the droning flies, and sense the overwhelming sensuality of the moment. Perhaps her arm would move and her hand touch his. She might begin to pull back, and then decide to leave it there. The electricity would flow sharp and detailed between their fingers. There would be a long low moment while decision hung in the air, and then slowly, deliberately, he would roll over, covering her body with his own, and bring his mouth down on her trembling lips.

'Are you making it with him?' I asked.

'Nothing's happened,' she said. 'We're just friends.' She paused. 'Do you want me to make it with him?'

Two currents ran through my mind. If I said 'yes' I would sever her in one stroke. But then I would have to live with that fantasy. And if I said 'no' I would be lying, because all I cared about was putting down the phone and getting back to Carol, and didn't really care what Regina did.

'Do what you want,' I said.

'All right,' she said. And then we hung up.

Conflicting emotions stormed beside me. How could it be possible to be jealous when there was no love, nor even any desire? It was not Regina as a person that bothered me, but the idea of Regina, Regina as a symbol. But a symbol of what?

The day passed in a jumble. And that night I went to one of those encounter groups which have become all the rage. I usually fled them like the pox, but I had run into Marsha, an old girl friend, the week before and she convinced me that her group was hip enough to be worth going to.

I had seen enough of the Esalen technique to be suspicious of anything having to do with programmed exposure. These workshops invariably involved the use of 'leaders', whose task it was to structure the physical and psychic environment in such a way as to predispose certain kinds of events. And within that, there was a forced unanimity of experience and expression that I could only honestly label as fascism. There was no doubt that the groups could turn people on, and even served as a medium for therapeutic insights. On occasion, as in the case of Fritz Perls, the individual was actually given a mirror in which to see himself more clearly. But hanging over all of these so-called growth centres was the spectre of Grossinger's, the suspicion that these were really fancy cruising grounds for the discontented middle class, and that for a stiff fee, people could come to feel and be felt, play head games, experience emotional catharsis, and in general indulge in a kind of open theatre. My major objection was that not one of these places had the honesty, humour, and historical perspective to see those aspects of their scene which were ludicrous, or dangerous, or merely degenerate partial residues of what once had simply been good living. Ultimately, it was the vulgarity of their instant intimacy and their putting a price on emotion which repelled me.

My masochism level had been running pretty low, so I dropped by the benefit weekend that Esalen held in New York City, where they raised over a hundred thousand dollars in two days by holding mass meetings of more than two thousand people at a time, leading them in ritualistic encounters. It was there I met Marsha, where she told me about her own group.

The two of us went out to smoke some grass, and then went back to prowl the halls and dig the scenes. We watched Esalen's chief guru arrive, unshaven, booze on his breath, and a cigarette hanging from his lips. In the great hall, some fifteen hundred people were told to 'close your eyes and go inside,' and then 'open your eyes and drink, drink in the face of your partner.' In another place a huge woman in a tent dress led a small army of people in group shouting. They all raised their arms in the air and chanted, 'I take responsibility for myself, I take responsibility for myself.' Then she read, and had them repeat, the Gestalt Prayer, which begins, 'You do your thing and I do mine.' The mixture of political form and pseudo-religious sentiment was making the air too thick to breathe. It was like watching a rally of psychic storm troopers, and I realised in a flash that Esalen was the Tibetan hierarchy of our time. They were setting the tone for the nation, and that no matter what kind of a revolution took place, no matter whether the right or the left took over, Esalen would remain privileged, giving massages and hot baths to the elite of whoever was in power.

We went into the lobby where several hundred people were smiling like crazy and embracing like socialist commissars of agriculture. Every now and then a real spark of sexuality would flare up, and the couple involved would jump back with a start, as though they suddenly realised that the touch-feely games they were playing had an actual basis in reality. These were the sensual counterparts of academic intellectuals. They liked to play with the notion of things, but ran like squirrels when the things themselves were made manifest. I had no real anger for the rubes who were spending seventy-five dollars each for a weekend of being processed through the superficial mill, hoping desperately for some magic to be rubbed off on them; but I was furious at the Esalen hucksters who blew into town to mop up a wad of money, promising visions of sensorial paradise and giving little more than two teenagers would find with each other on a date in the park. Lonely men, lonely women, husbands who no longer wanted to fuck their wives and wives with dried-up cunts, all of them milling around with bright gazes, and leaning postures, wanting to be picked up, wanting to be plugged in, preying on the vibrations – this was the emotional cul-de-sac of a dying civilisation. And it fit the proper historical ironic mode that as Americans, they didn't even have the style and passion to make real orgies. Even decadence had become plastic.

I left in disgust, a thousand 'groovies' ringing in my ears, and made a date to go to Marsha's group. The night I arrived there, I was pleasantly surprised to find that all the people were sitting around as though they lived there. There were four women and five men, including myself and the leader. It is odd to use the word to describe Larry, because he didn't 'run' the group; he simply served as its focus and let the energy find its own forms.

Nothing spectacular happened. We rapped a bit, and a few of us told our stories. At one point we got into a massage thing, and just enjoyed solid physical contact with one another. I flashed on two of the chicks, and the three of us got into one of those circles, with arms around each other's shoulders, heads touching, and each of us moaning Om to dig the group vibration. I realised that

I was playing the Esalen games, but this was something we came upon easily and spontaneously. There was no social director telling us where to put our hands when, and suggesting what we should feel. It was just people getting into each other.

When the group ended, Al offered to drive the three of us downtown, since he was on his way to Brooklyn. Joyce and Connie and I piled in, and halfway there, I asked them over. They agreed, and in a short while we were spilling into my apartment, with a surprised Carol greeting us at the door.

Carol was in an odd mood that night and immediately split to the kitchen, where she began typing and yelling to herself. The others, not knowing her, were uncomfortable with this particular expression of insanity. We smoked some dope and put on some music, and settled into an easy rhythm. The talk turned to sex, and the mood turned to sex. And suddenly the proposition was hanging palpably in the air, and no one could pretend not to see it. Connie looked at the rest of us and said, 'Are we all going to ball together, is that it?' We nodded quiet assent, and while the three of them began taking their clothes off, I went into the bedroom to bring out a mattress.

When I returned the three of them were standing awkwardly. This was another of those times when there was greater interest in the fact of the act than in the act itself. I imagine we were taken by the idea of an orgy, while the orgy itself seemed a mere vehicle for the theatre we had in mind. I put the mattress down, undressed, and the four of us sank to the floor. I turned to Joyce and Al took Connie in his arms. Joyce was about thirty-five, and she look as though she had been through all the scenes, the kind of chick who starts the evening by getting pissed on in the shower and takes off from there. Her breasts had the sag and stretched skin of a woman her age, and her cunt was totally raunchy, with pendulous lips that seemed permanently bruised. I couldn't begin to imagine how many cocks had been inside her. We wasted no time on any preliminaries. She lay back and opened her legs; she was already wet. I moved on top of her and plunged right into her pussy. It was an immediate turn-on. Her experienced cunt began to surge inside and grip my cock, massaging it as she pushed her pelvis onto me. She closed her eyes and her mouth dropped open. I put my fingers between her lips and she started biting and sucking them, moaning in a low purring sound.

I looked to the right and saw Al's large bulk lower itself onto Connie's thin body. Connie was one of those chicks who put up a kind of super-ficial defence against fucking, but once they are into it, let go completely. She didn't have orgasms in the conventional sense, no great surging come, but rather a continual rippling opening, a sensual movement of the cunt that seemed like a dance and could go on for hours. She was best when a man had one of those fatigue hard-ons, when there is no real urge to come, but a low-level excitement which keeps the cock hard. Then her cunt was like a mindless mouth, feeling the cock churn inside her, reaming every inch of her pussy. She didn't get very wet, but gave off enough lubrication to keep the slit tight and slippery. Now she brought her knees to her chest and exposed her cunt fully. She looked up at Al, who began grunting and banging his weight into her. 'Oh fuck it, fuck it baby, fuck my cunt,' she said. At her words, Joyce turned on and started to grab my ass to pull me deeper into her.

For a while the four of us rode like that, Al working his tool into Connie and me sloshing around in Joyce's brimming twat. And then Carol walked into the room. She seemed frantic and went about pointedly ignoring us, although we were aware that she was totally aware of us. It presented a slightly surrealistic picture, and the four of us continued our movement, but with a kind of suspended animation, as though we were waiting to see what Carol would do. For a moment I imagined she might join us, and then, to my astonishment, she switched on the television.

An old Western came on, and the sound of cattle thundering across a prairie assailed our ears. It was too funny, and we began laughing. At that, Carol let out a yipping yell and went tearing back into the kitchen where she started pounding furiously at her typewriter once more.

We all looked at one another, shrugged our shoulders, and started in again. This time I was ready to come. I reached over and put one hand on Connie's breast, and began to massage her nipple. She moaned and spread her legs wider for Al to sink into her. Joyce had gone catatonic. She was just lying back, ready to take whatever I gave her, letting her cunt be an open receptacle, trading movement for sensation. I turned my attention to her and wondered again at the nature of the woman. No matter how old or young, how sophisticated or naive, no matter what race or education or situation, when it came right down to it, woman was just cunt. When she took the cock inside her, she became most what she essentially is, the vessel, the chalice for the sperm of life. And the body and personality attached to the cunt are simply the trappings, the nicety of setting.

The two women crying out, Al working furiously to ream Connie's cunt, and me swimming in Joyce's experienced box, we pumped and thrust until I could feel Joyce rippling under me, and my cock answered the call by summoning the sperm up from my balls and shooting it wildly into her. At that, she jerked her whole body forward, grabbed onto my shoulders, and sucked at my cock with her pussy as the orgasm raked the inside of her body. Simultaneously, Connie threw her legs completely back, so that her ankles were practically at her knees, and then grabbed her feet with her hands and spread them apart. Her legs

211

made a wide split V, and she looked like a diver doing a somersault off the high board. Al came up on his toes so his entire torso was off the floor, and he crashed into her, her sobbing and loving the punishment. He started to make a coughing grunting sound, and pumped harder and harder until he lost all control of his body flopped and convulsed into her like a great fish jerked up on land. She took him all in, pulling the cock, drawing the sperm deeply into her, stretching her body as wide as she could to engulf him entirely. He came for a long time, and then subsided and sank onto her. She wrapped her legs around him and licked his throat and face, running her hands up and down his spine and taking handfuls of flesh to pinch and pummel.

Finally she too stopped, and the four of us lay quiet and breathing hard. Just then Carol came rushing through the room headed for the door and went tittering out into the hall and downstairs. Joyce looked up, startled. 'What's that?' she said. 'What's wrong with her?' demanded Connie. I smiled. 'Oh, she's just tripping on her own tonight,' I said. 'She's all right.'

We rearranged ourselves and lit some more joints. The first round had been powerful but short, and we needed to digest what had happened before we'd be ready for second helpings. I put on some music and we sat in silence, smoking, listening to it. Connie and I got into an eye dance, with all the glimmerings and half-meanings being

212

suggested in our glances and facial gestures. She began to breathe harder and leaned toward me, her breasts hanging forward. I dropped my reefer and bent down under her breasts, turned my face up, and took one of the swaying orbs totally into my mouth. She gasped and pulled my head harder against her. Simultaneously, Al reached from behind and held her other breast in his hand. She let out a low moan and simply sank back, totally passive. I moved onto her, sucking at her nipple, while Al pummelled her breast and brought his mouth down on hers. Gradually her movements became more frantic, and something was happening with her which seemed more than what Al and I were providing. Then I looked down and saw Joyce, lying long between Connie's legs, her mouth glued to her cunt, sucking greedily and noisily.

Connie seemed to have forgotten about us and was centering all her concentration on her crotch. I stopped what I was doing and sat back to watch. Joyce was nuzzling and burrowing into the cunt, licking and slurping as though the thing could actually be eaten. Then she grabbed the cunt lips with her teeth, and began gnawing on them. Connie began to scream, not a yell of pain but a kind of cry of joyous anguish, as though what was happening to her were too much to bear. Joyce put both her hands between the cunt lips and pried them open, and then dove into the exposed centre, again thrusting her tongue in and out, cupping it to lap up the juices. Connie was letting out gasping moans when suddenly Joyce covered the entire cunt with her lips and began sucking her breath in. She was creating a vacuum in Connie's cunt, sucking out the air, making the walls collapse. Connie grabbed my arm with one hand and dug her nails into the flesh, all the while grunting 'Ungh, ungh, ungh,' and rolling her head from side to side. Then, with a startling swiftness, Joyce pulled a lungful of air through her nostrils and blew it forcibly into Connie's pussy. Connie seemed to explode. The cry which came from her didn't sound human, and her arms and legs flailed out like a sky diver's during free fall. Joyce reversed the action and sucked all the air out of her cunt again, and again blew in, doing it again and again until Connie became a mass of quivering protoplasm, babbling mindlessly, drooling, hiccuping.

Suddenly Al moved. He snaked quickly down next to Joyce and pulled her back roughly by the shoulder, and sank his face between Connie's legs. He went at it with a will, but when he used his teeth he really bit, coming down hard on the sensitive cunt lips. Connie began pounding the floor with her fists, and thrusting her cunt into his face, urging him to ravish her more. I moved up and dropped my cock into her mouth. She sucked at it like a baby on a rubber nipple. When it was hard I pulled out and hurled myself toward Joyce, who was kneeling over watching Al eat Connie's cunt. I took her from behind and fucked her for a long time, watching the cunt lips pull in and push out as my cock slid back and forth along the slimy track.

Then there was a kind of pause, and Al came up from his feast and I pulled out of Joyce. He looked at us, and I turned Joyce around, offering him her ass and cunt. He didn't hesitate for a moment, and shoved his large tool into the steaming crack. Joyce took it without seeming to notice that it was a different man inside her now; she just leaned back into him and let him fuck her. I moved onto Connie and thrust into her defenceless cunt. She had no resistance, no tension, I drove all the way up past her cervix the first time, and lodged there. Her legs came up, and the tip of my cock snuggled even deeper into the back folds of her box. Then, bracing my feet on the floor, I began rooting and scooping into her, using my cock like a drill, as though I were trying to break through the back wall of the vagina. Her mouth opened and she froze. The sensation seemed to have reached a level where she could no longer move, but just hang in there and let it happen. The heat inside her was astonishing; I felt as though my cock were being fried.

Then Joyce crept forward, Al coming behind her, walking on his knees, keeping his cock inside her. She moved up level with Connie's body, and lowered her mouth onto Connie's stretched lips. Her tongue slithered out and completely filled

Connie's mouth. She ground into her, mashing her lips against the other lips, thrusting her tongue again and again into Connie's throat, until Connie began to respond, climbing slowly out of her stupor to give back the kisses she was receiving. Then the two of them began a dance of lips and tongues, wetly covering each other's mouth and chin, sucking and licking. At the same time Al began to drive harder into Joyce's cunt, which hung wetly under her upturned ass. I started to feel the heat rising in my groin.

In a moment, a strange transformation took place. We all knew that we were approaching orgasm, and we all knew that we knew. It was one of those dangerously self-conscious moments when you know something is going perfectly and will continue to do so unless the thought-machine begins producing distractions in the mind. We hung on the balance of our awareness, and kept free of all fantasies. Al and I drove harder and the two women kissed more passionately. The tension grew, and the quotient of release increased. I now felt as though I were driving right into Connie's belly, and Al hit at Joyce's cheeks like a pile-driver. We rode and rode, higher and heavier, until all four of us stiffened at once, and then let the floodgates burst open, as Al and I shot our loads into our respective women, and the women bucked under us, coming, and moaning into one another's mouths.

There was a general collapse and we all lay

there, still and quiet. Suddenly the door opened and Carol came in again. She had five ice cream cones and breezed into the room like the zany wife in the TV situation comedies. 'Ooh,' she said, 'I hope our guests are having a good time.' For all the corniness of it, the humour was genuine, and we all began laughing. Carol bustled among us, handing out the cones, and we gradually sat up, one by one, like children at a picnic.

Carol went back into the kitchen and in a few seconds we heard the typewriter clacking again. 'Ooh, what a story I'm writing about you,' she called out.

Suddenly, I realised what was happening. We had come in as a group, the orgy having been forming for some time in our minds. Carol greeted us without a context, and was thrown into confusion. She didn't feel she could join us, and yet didn't know how to be delicately unobtrusive. So, consciously or not, she hit upon the brilliant notion of acting totally zany, figuring that a featherhead would be the least threatening to the vibrations. My admiration and liking for her went up immensely, and I couldn't help comparing her to Regina, for whom this kind of scene would have been a crushing trauma, and who would either have asked everyone to leave, or gone off to sulk very loudly.

It seemed that a part of mind slid open and I saw my entire relationship with Regina in a new light and now I couldn't even remember what it was about her that had attracted me so violently for so long. I pictured her face in my mind, and like a lightning streak I remembered a picture of my mother when she was thirty. Of course, she and Regina could have been twins. I didn't see it because my mother had grown so much older and heavier, with grey hair.

I began to laugh. The simplicity of it almost reduced it to the banal. Like all modern men, I had become an Oedipus who could only deal with the reality symbolically. Instead of fucking my mother, I chose a woman who reminded me of her when she was young and most beautiful, and when I was at an age to be imprinted with her looks and my feelings for her at the time. The mists burned away from my eyes and I felt as I do in therapy when some revelation comes crashing home and a great load of confusion and anxiety is removed.

I got up and went into the kitchen. Carol stopped her typing and looked up at me. Her face was split into the opposing feelings of doubt and warmth. I looked deep into her eyes and the communication that passed between us erased all her doubts.

I went over and took her in my arms. What I was feeling right then couldn't be called love. Rather it was a sort of friendship and intimacy that transcended all attempts to describe or explain it. We both knew, and knew that we knew, and there was no 'what' to confuse the pure act of knowing.

When I went back in, the others were dressing. I offered to have them spend the night, but they all wanted to leave. There was a polite exchange of farewells and they went off. I turned from the door to see Carol standing there, now naked. She came up and took me by the hand and led me to the bedroom. I let myself be led in, and lay on top of her when she threw herself on the bed.

I held her tightly in my arms and felt the familiar curves of her. I felt my cock begin to stir, painful though it was. Carol looked at me, smiled a warning smile, and said, 'You'd better have enough left for me.'

My heart filled with affection for her. She was able to take in the entire evening, handle it magnificently, assimilate it, and then come back to me without any of her feelings diminished or distorted. All she wanted was me, but in a very clean, open way. There was no hidden clause concerning my sexual fidelity or any exclusiveness with her.

Then I understood what I could never get clear with Regina, that specialness between two human beings is always an ad hoc contract. It is made on pure impulse, and has no justification other than its own existence. When either or both of the parties feel it disappear or drive it away, then it no longer exists, and there can be no recriminations. Also, it has nothing to say about sexual activity with others. Somehow, between two people, a special kind of flow is possible, and when that is there, there are no rules about anything else. All is clear.

And the people who just left were not demeaned by it. They were part of the new international brotherhood and sisterhood of sexual journeymen, people who could enjoy the sexual act fully upon first meeting, because their heads were in a place that allows fullness without the intervening struggle. This was not to obviate the beautiful richness that grows between two people who are with each other a long time, but to suggest that there was an alternative between promiscuity and fidelity. It involved an ability to adapt to very rapid, very heavy changes, very quickly, and hang in for the ride without either getting unconscious or freaking out.

My now hard cock slipped into Carol's cunt, and I was home. We fucked simply and warmly, without any special trips, just experiencing each other and letting all our need and fear and love hang out. We pumped steadily into one another, letting our climax build slowly and regularly, savouring the climb, kissing and caressing each other along the way. Her breasts crushed against my chest, her mouth on mine, her ass a soft engine moving her cunt into me, I felt myself in paradise. Not a sexual paradise, but a paradise of fucking, where that ultimate and terribly final act attained its total purity.

To fuck, this is all we know and all we derive from. The rest is food, clothing, and shelter. And all the accomplishments of our civilisations, every last work of religion or art or science, has been nothing but a frippery to pass the time away, to keep oneself busy while one was not doing the only thing in which human beings achieve totality: fucking.

Our breaths became as one, our moans mingled, our bodies yearned toward each other, and as the sperm rolled up the tube and spurted burningly into her, her cunt grabbed my cock and rippled again and again onto it, as she spent herself joyously and openly.

Unconsciousness followed soon after, and my last thought before sleep was a vision of a Buddhist Valhalla, a Nirvana of the Koran, where woman, eternal woman, lay in smiling understanding and possession of everything that poor scrambling man spends all his days searching for.

(11)

YET THE PROBLEM was merely more clearly defined. To change from Regina to Carol was no solution in and of itself. What had to be guarded against was falling into the same kinds of dynamics which had strangled me in the earlier relationship. I wondered what would happen if the scene of the night of the orgy was reversed, and Carol were to come home with some people and begin fucking on the living room floor. At this point, I wouldn't mind, but if that kind of possessive clinging set in, I would once again be prey to jealousy. Yet the more I opened to Carol, the more vulnerable I became. Obviously the thing I was looking for lay in my attitude toward the relationship, for the relationship is always the same.

I threw the *I Ching*, and it came up with Preponderance of the Great, changing to The Joyous, Lake. The *Ching* is a psychic Rorschach. It begins with basic dualities and ramifies them, so that a complete system of applications to practical situations is presented in language that is at once abstract and concrete. The gist of the oracle was that there was a danger of too much concentration in the centre without enough support for the weight. This indicated to me that I had to be careful not to saturate myself in the experience of Carol past my ability to assimilate what was happening. The changing line read: 'The ridgepole sags to the breaking point. Misfortune. This indicates the type of man who in times of the preponderance of the great insists on pushing ahead. He accepts no advice from others, and therefore they in turn are not willing to lend him support. Because of this the burden grows, until the structure of things bends or breaks. Plunging wilfully ahead in times of danger only hastens the catastrophe.'

One of the things I love about *The Book of Changes* is its steadfast refusal to get fancy or esoteric. It describes the human condition in the most mundane terms, and through that achieves universality. It seemed that I was being advised to be cautious, not to get carried away by the enthusiasm engendered during the Preponderance of the Great. I turned to the second hexagram and read: 'True joy, therefore, rests on firmness

226

and strength within, manifesting itself outwardly as yielding and gentle.' And again, 'Lakes resting one on the other: the image of the Joyous. Thus the Superior Man joins with his friends for discussion and practice.' The explanation of the Image ran: 'A lake evaporates upward and thus gradually dries up; but when two lakes are joined they do not dry up so readily, for one replenishes the other. It is the same in the field of knowledge. Knowledge should be a refreshing and vitalising force. It becomes so only through stimulating intercourse with congenial friends with whom one holds discussion and practices application of the truths of life. In this way learning becomes many-sided and takes on a cheerful lightness, whereas there is always something ponderous and one-sided about the learning of the self-taught.'

It isn't wise to try to wrest too literal interpretations from the oracle. Rather, its words should be allowed to sink into the mind, there to suggest openings to the truth of a situation. The *I Ching* is not, as S. I. Hayakawa construed it, 'A Chinese fortune-telling book.' Still, the temptation is strong to make practical applications, and what the text seemed to be saying was, that Carol's and my relationship would succeed to the degree that we hung loose in the beginning, and then moved into a mutuality which fed and supported us in our life together. And this sharing had to be based on a reverence for learning. It was very Confucian in its overtones, and I marvelled again at the almost seamless blend between that and the older Taoist mode of appreciating reality which permeates the book.

The immediate problem now was disposing of Regina, and when I put it to myself in those terms, I felt brutal about it. Yet I could put no more accurate face on it. The woman was an encumbrance in her demand for permanence, and while I had been as guilty as she in sharing the desire, I had found another person with whom to try the experiment. That was simply the way of things.

Perhaps the most accurate description of love/marriage affairs was given by Reich when he spoke of 'serial monogamy.' His notion is that there occurs a bio-energetic flow between human beings which expresses itself most fully in the sexual act, where the energies are exchanged, reinforce themselves, and culminate in orgasm. So long as this flow is full, the 'marriage' is successful. But when it fails, for whatever reason, in one or the other or both, the bond is broken. But instead of separating cleanly, the people concerned get embroiled in recriminations, problems of responsibility and support, and, if there are children, in guilt. But the dead cannot be revived, and so much of what is pathetic in human relationship is the attempt to rekindle a flame that has gone out. The alternative is to be sophisticated, to keep the marriage as a shell of convenience, to hold the home and hearth together, and then both swing freely in and out of that contest, taking lovers and reducing the bond to a mere social arrangement. It was a mode I privately referred to as 'the French solution.'

So the letter to Regina was composed, candidly, even harshly. It contained several hundred words, but the single message was NO. This time there was no hesitation or second-thought phone calls. I simply mailed it, and with that action, erased Regina from my life. She was now one of many partners of the past, with whom I had shared part of my life, and from whom I derived much, as well as giving much. I felt an incredible lightness and clarity of purpose, as though some inner purpose had been set. I recalled Wittgenstein's words, 'I am resolved, but I do not know to what.'

I spent some time appraising my situation, both in itself and in relation to Carol. Metaphysically, I was on a here-and-now trip, paying no attention to yesterday and treating tomorrow as a sketchy outline within which I would manoeuver. I had no absolutes, merely working hypotheses, and these were of a nature that to formulate them was to destroy them. I also realised that Sartre was right: one defines oneself by the act, not by the thought about the act. So, before anything could be understood in terms of Carol's and my relationship, I would have to make an inner commitment to our scene. And it would have to be as open as possible while containing parameters to define it.

I sat at the typewriter and drew up a contract of marriage, one which would contain, mostly by

implication, all the 'rules' I felt were important.
It ran as follows:

CONTRACT OF MARRIAGE

I am on a mysterious trip somewhere in the
unknown. I walk lightly between the pit of sterility and the quagmire of insanity. My only
means to health is to maintain order within
myself, and let the externals find their own
form.

The only necessary relation to the Absolute
is simple recognition. You may be my mate for
so long as you wish to stay with me, me as I
am at any given point in spacetime or otherwise.

I signed it and delivered it to Carol. Her reaction was quite odd. She simultaneously appreci-
ated it warmly, and was sarcastic about it. I
realised with a start that I was beginning to see
her very acutely, coming to, as the common
phrase has it, 'understand her.' It astonished me
to see our relationship in this manner. I was
observing myself observe myself in relationship to
another entity, this woman. I got an immediate
schizophrenic high, and the words of my Gurdjieff
guru came thundering home: 'You must be serious
about the Work. If you fuck with it, it will chew
you up.'

Carol read it, went through her changes, and
said to me: 'What's the scene?' I said: 'Dig it, I'm

a male lesbian and you're a dyke, a butch, not a femme. But we dig mostly the other sex. What we need to complete this is a mature femme. I could get from her the softness I miss in you. You could get from her the chance to assert authority, which you can't do with me. From me, she would receive a masculinity sensitive and gentle enough not to frighten her, and we would make beautiful love together. From you she would get the support for her image, a support she truly needs. And the two of you would make beautiful love to each other. And you and I would receive the benefit of having given ourselves a gist for one another. And on rare brilliant moments, the three of us would understand ourselves as one.'

'That's a nice picture,' she said. 'It doesn't work that way.'

'Of course it doesn't,' I said, 'because those who wish to enter that state are not willing to do the hard work necessary to live there. Make no mistake; it is not easy. But the question is, 'how do you choose to lead your life?'

We looked at one another in a moment such as the Tibetans describe when they say, 'to come face to face with the Nakedness.' There was a shock of recognition which bordered on horror, and sheer terror gripped us. We dis-located. There was, for that instant, no parameter within which to understand the moment. Total strangeness ensued. The universe got nauseous.

And then the attack subsided. She seemed

frightened. I remembered the words of Steve Gaskin, and they entered my heart to sustain me. He said: 'On the astral plane, I share the weather with everybody else.' Of course, that's all that was happening: an astral storm brewing. And the two of us were in the same boat. So the thing for us to do was to hold on to each other, and help each other to weather the blast. We moved into one another's arms, and at the touch of her flesh on mine, a sweet warmth flooded me. Now let the winds blow, we are safe in one another's arms.

Tears came to my eyes. It was so beautiful to trust this human being, to let myself be totally vulnerable in my need for her, recognising that she was wracked by the very same need. We held each other. That is, *neither* of us had anything to hold onto except the other. And I remembered the Doré drawing of Paolo and Francesca in the Fifth Circle of the Inferno, how they tenderly touched one another, and were born aloft on a white diaphanous cloud. And when she told her story, she wept in such a manner that all the strength of Paolo could not comfort her. And that was their punishment. In the face of that, Sartre's *No Exit* is a gross and flatulent conception.

Of course, with these thoughts, the paranoia returned. Was I indeed stepping into my projected romantic hell, that delightful Shavian Underworld? The warmth of her belly burning into mine dispelled all that. And I felt her pubic hair brush mine, as she moved her cunt into me. She held it at a barely touching distance for a long time, letting the dance of her pubic hair on mine feed our genitals and asses and bowels with sensation, and the beginning of a glowing heat. I took her breasts in my hands, those beautiful, warm, life-sustaining, pendulous, sensitive and holy breasts, which at the same time were so lascivious, so inviting of plunder, so defenceless and so central to that which is a woman. I have often thought that a woman's sex life is in her cunt, but where she lives is what's hanging from her chest.

Then, as I rubbed her nipples and bent down to bite them, more than a little hard, she buckled at the waist and moaned. She fell into my arms. I savaged at her breast, biting and giving high intensity pleasure/pain, keeping it always at the edge while escalating the charge up to its very limit before exploding. I thought, upon thinking this, that I should be in command of the army in Vietnam. I suddenly flashed myself as a Five-Star General, and all the fascist fantasies, all those marvelous Triumph of the Will manifestos, surged in me. For a moment I became Hitler.

Carol crushed her pubic bone into mine. Fiercely, we rubbed them together, generating the spark, or, to use the Freudian model, priming the pump. She brought the bone down to the top of my cock, right at the place where it hangs suspended from the skin of my belly. It is the spot where manual massage will get even the laziest cock hard. Now, with that pressure, and the heat

233

coming from her cunt, my cock stiffened, and positioned itself between her thighs. We gasped at the experience.

Now, I'm the kind of guy that gets downright Tibetan at times. Suddenly the entire universe became manifest in terms of this moment. CLONG! it went in my head. This moment . . . this moment . . . THIS MOMENT. It was always this moment, and this moment was always the same, but different; the same, but wider; the same, but now. And the now flowed, creating a river of time in eternity.

I stepped back, we looked into one another's eyes. What happened is inexpressible, but immense amounts of meaning suddenly fell into place. I remembered Bob Fishman, Fish we used to call him, who was the most beautiful dealer the world has ever seen, and he died at thirty-three of something wrong in his brain, just six months after he was saying to me, out of a twenty-day acid jag, 'You know, I feel as though I'm headed towards some involuntary sacrifice of myself.'

I had looked at him, the Jewish intellectual head hero from Minnesota, with a family of acid farmers, living pure communism in Oregon, and realised that he had spent four years with Starling, the woman I had spent eleven months with, Aquarius to Scorpio, and that she was a Christian, and poor Bob was living out the Christ story. Ah, but how many people he turned on, and in such a beautiful, sweet way! I remembered him sitting in a car in the Fillmore, his contact going into one of the buildings in the black neighbourhood to pick up a few pounds of hash, and all around us in hallways are real mean-looking fuckers, and coolness must prevail. Across the street was a cop's car, its roof light flashing. And we tried to appear nonchalant. And Fish and I shared a buzzing electrical moment of existential criminality. Then he turned to me and said, 'Yeah, I like to be where the action is.' And later, after we had successfully scored, saying: 'I've reduced it all to three things: dope, chicks, and meaning.'

I blessed him in my heart, for he was still alive in me. And I stood with this young, giving, smart, beautiful woman, and wondered whether I dare make a commitment to myself concerning her.

O what a life this was! The same fucking eternal enigmas always returned at precisely this moment, just when everything had seemed so clear. It was the necessity of choice that made the problem acute, and not merely academic. I remembered the words of Engels: *Freedom is the recognition of necessity*. And those of Krishnamurti: *What is necessary is choiceless awareness, that's all*.

At such moments of turmoil the first thing I reach for is chronological time. I looked at the clock. It was five-fifteen. It was afternoon. It was Spring. I was in New York City. On the planet Earth. I remembered my name.

I stepped back, and looked at Carol while remembering myself. I could no longer con myself. The truth was manifest, and I had to cop to it. I would always be living in this moment, making this decision, understanding this mystery. It was like the Sufi story of The Eternal Return. Only, the Sufis knew something the existentialists don't. They refer to that which returns as: The Friend.

(12)

FATIGUE! MY EYES burned in marble-eyed staring. I had lost all sense of my body as a biological organism. I had been up for fifty-two hours, and all of that time spent locked in the house with Carol. One night, after getting very stoned and fucking, I was suddenly overwhelmed by a wave of total despair. Yet it brought with it a peace, a kind of quietude which was like a balm. I understood my total worthlessness in a stroke, and for the first time was able to take a total breath without the feeling that I had to prove something by breathing.

It was two weeks after Carol moved in, and this brings the story to a close. After our night of mutual revelation, we honeymooned for five days.

There was not a word, a gesture, an idea that either of us could create which the other could find fault with. Every smile, every roll of her hips, her quirks, even her farts, were precious to me. And time and time again we would find ourselves looking deep into one another's eyes, until we became aware of what was happening, and became embarrassed.

The head tripping we did was phenomenal. And the fucking became phantasmagorical. It was like pure acid, but mostly we were stoned on grass and truth, a winning combination every time. The house seemed to be filled with people every afternoon and evening, while we had the nights and mornings to ourselves. How dear this little madwoman became. I pictured us a George Burns and Gracie Allen. It was a vacation, I didn't care what happened. It was all dizzying and glorious. I stopped doing hatha yoga in the mornings, I went up to almost three packs of cigarettes a day, I became skinny. I slept no more than five hours a night. And I hadn't felt so healthy, alive, and clear-headed in a very long time.

Then the dam burst, and the energies which had been whirling through the cyclotron of my consciousness brimmed and spilled over, and suddenly it was as though the atomic pile had been activated, and the whole reactor was about to explode. It is difficult to describe such moments

240

to those who have not experienced them. It is as though the mind becomes a vacuum and the entire universe, real and conceptual, comes roaring in in a single rush. It often results in unconsciousness, or panic; but sometimes it turns into a speed satori. All elements of fantasy and reality are kept in a constant dizzying rapid dance like swords flung in the air by a juggler. The situation becomes so complex, and the rate of events and their realisations is so fast, that one must forget all about attempting to use skill to keep everything from crashing down; one goes into no-mind overdrive, and follows the Tao which, a pleasant stream a while back, had suddenly become a thundering cascade of white whipping water.

The fucking we did the night the double all-nighter began was very bad. I couldn't scrape up enough sperm to satisfy an artificial insemination bank. My cock was so sore that it hurt to get a full erection. The hole in the tip was red and chafed. But lust still bubbled in my belly, and I attempted to rouse my cock to yet another round.

But, for about the twentieth time in my life, the organ rebelled. It said, 'Fuck fucking, I've had enough.' Carol was ready to be turned on, but wasn't really hot yet. We played a few desultory foreplay games and subsided. In all honesty, I wanted to sleep, but I saw Carol's breasts lolling around on her chest, and her cunt making very small motions, and I began again. This time, as she lay, legs spread apart, knees up, I began trailing my fingers up and down the insides of her thighs, causing little shudders to run over her skin. I traced a meandering path to her cunt area, and tickled and teased all around the lips, especially in the most sensitive spot between the cunt lips and the crack which separates crotch from thigh, the place where the pubic hair is thinner and finer, where a kiss is felt reverberating through the entire body.

Then gently and with increasing speed, I began spanking her cunt, tapping against it with my fingertips and cupping it with the palm of my hand, letting it call out and into me. I pressed my knuckles against the tender blades of flesh and slowly inserted one finger into the opening. I kept it at the very bud, the pink closed door to the inner delights. Her cunt began sucking at my finger. I don't know how she did it, but there was a definite engorging taking place, as though she were a fish gaping at food. I could feel the grainy passage contract, pull my finger inside, and then relax and open again. Each time she did it my finger was drawn in further, until I was reaching into her deepest part and riding out the small convulsions taking place in her pussy. She became very wet, and my finger made sloshing sounds as I brought it back and forth, in and out of that enchanting lower mouth.

I got up and hung over her, supported by one hand, balancing on my toes, and brought my cock up to her cunt. I placed it right next to the finger still moving inside her, and as I pulled my finger out, I slipped my cock in. To use the vernacular, it was all peaches and cream. Sweet salvation of pussy! Creamy deliciousness of soulful cunt! Oh beautiful ladychild of the eternal randiness! I cupped her cheeks in my hands, and then the changes began.

The first thought that came to mind was Carol's story that she had been a hooker for a night, and on another occasion had been used and beaten up by a pimp. I noticed now, as she fucked, that she had only put her right leg around my left leg, and was pushing her other hip up and down. It became obvious that she was not only a hooker, but that she hooked to the right! I let the political implications of that pass, and concentrated on the sociology of the phenomenon.

It gave her great control over her movements. One leg was braced against the wall, while the other served as a lever. The weight being lifted was her right hip, and the fulcrum was her cunt. But it was not a stationary fulcrum; it moved and surged, it pleased and demanded. She was able to move her cunt onto my cock from an infinity of directions, and then have it penetrate as deeply or lightly as she wanted. She could ripple the inside of her vagina, and would shift the angle of her pelvis to send me thrusting into different levels of heat at the core of her cunt.

I began to indulge in the prostitute fantasy, treating her as an object, as a person who had no

243

essential worth except in terms of her masochism and passion. I plied both sides of that psychic street. And of course, she went wild behind it. In acting the way I was, I allowed her to take her own trip fully. There was no way of knowing whether her fantasy reciprocated mine, for that happens quite often. But our bodies moved in perfect harmony, and that's what seemed of most importance.

Then, she surged up, brought her entire cunt up off the bed, and offered it wholly to my penetrating, ravaging cock. I fucked straight into her. And she began to writhe, to grip my cock with that churning tunnel, and demand the sperm from it. She was sucking me off with her pussy, insisting that I come in her symbolic mouth (or is a mouth a symbolic cunt?). At just that moment, my faithful tool went soft. The pressure was too much for even its brave heart, and it collapsed into half its erect size. Carol didn't seem to notice. At this point, as long as there was minimal penetration, the feeling of pubic bone hitting clitoris, and the thrashing of a male body above her, she could climb her own stairs to orgasm. But as she grew in heat and intensity, I shrank from her need. I went from being the dominant thrusting force to a shrinking and meek failure. Impotence had struck again!

Paradoxically, at that moment I went into Reichian spasms, the vegetative energy making my spine ripple and my pelvis shudder rapidly. I went with the flow and felt myself bucking in her arms and fucking her cunt with spontaneous movements. She did something very rare for her; she threw her legs into the air and let me have the full view of her upturned exposed pink twat, begging me to penetrate it right to the pit. And I had nothing to effect the penetration with.

I cursed myself and just sank into her arms, spent. She went through rapid changes and then relaxed, letting me drift into her. If I had had any sense at that point, I would have just slipped into sleep. But I felt as though I had some kind of debt to pay, some obscure bond I had to meet. And so I got off her, lay by her side, and began fondling her breasts. My action was so contrived, so mechanical and unfeeling, that she was immediately turned off to it. I hit the panic button; the one thing I had been able to count on with Carol was the fact that I could turn her on at will, any time. And now even that was failing. It should be clear that by this time perspective had fled over the horizon of anxiety.

I lay back, and silently begged her to go down on me. But I suppose the astral plane was socked in with fog and she didn't respond. So I subsided, and we lay there a long time. Slowly she began massaging my thighs, working her hand up to my hips, across my belly, and down into my pubic hair. She worked all the way to the base of my cock, stopped, and removed her hand. She repeated the cycle a dozen times, each time grab-

245

bing the cock for longer periods of time. It was maddening. She was toying with me and my head was in a place where I could see it was real. I didn't have the energy to direct her in any way. I could only lie there and hope she would be good to me. After the last time around, there was a long, long silence, and then, decisively, she moved her mouth down to my cock. I smiled with relief, and awaited the blow job with tingling anticipation. The wet warm engulfment took the head of my cock into itself, and I felt myself melting into the sensations. She worked as though her mouth were filled with glue. It was a slowly, sticky kind of cocksucking, and totally delicious.

I let her suck me like that for what seemed almost a half hour, enjoying the sight of her lips stretched over the hard flesh pole, and the way her ass moved as she sucked, and the tickling of her fingers at my balls. Finally, when I sensed her tiring of it, I brought her up to me, turned her over, and penetrated again into her cunt.

This time she was cold to me. She turned her face to the side. And her cunt moved mechanically, ruthlessly. I let her vent her rage, riding out the rough storm, and when she began to become exhausted, I picked up her rhythm and carried it for her. This set off the spark which triggered the explosion. We exchanged roles back and forth a number of times, and then I began kissing her cheeks, pulling at them with my lips to bring her mouth around. She resisted, and suddenly I remembered the story that whores would never let you kiss them on the lips, My experience had been almost exclusively with Japanese whores, so I didn't know whether the story was statistically correct or an apocryphal myth. But my imagination cared not at all for such sophistries. What would it be like to have a whore give up her mouth? I wondered. It would be a kind of offering of virginity.

I moved her face to face mine. She squeezed her eyes shut and refused to let her lips get soft. I lowered my mouth to hers and began kissing her gently. At first, she did not respond, but then began to acknowledge the kisses, and then to return them. Her lips parted and she moaned, a short gasping sound. Then I brought my cock into focus, screwing it into her in a helical swirl. Her cunt and entire pelvis shifted around the motion, like water in a balloon which is jiggled from below.

The action at our mouths and the action at our groins conjoined, and suddenly we were fucking in both places at once. What happened in her cunt was reflected by her tongue, and what happened to her lips found an echo in her cunt. Soon we were exchanging deep, passionate kisses, groaning and slobbering over one another, and then pulling back to let our mouths barely touch so that our breaths could commingle.

She moved her body faster, now really hitting her cunt into me. Her mouth was totally wanton, holding nothing back, letting itself take its full trip. We blended, and we headed toward climax. There was no hesitation now, no fear. This was the home stretch and we were running neck and neck, running well. Oddly, it was as though we could already see the finish line we were heading toward. And while this robbed the act of its mystery, it infused it with an equally powerful intelligence.

I recalled Jim Morrison's words, 'This is the end, beautiful friend . . . no safety or surprise, the end . . . I'll never look into your eyes again.' Orgasm was simply that point on the matrix where our curves crossed and we died to ourselves and one another. It was a phase to be gone through and, phenomenologically, it was merely of a different texture from other experiences, but not more significant. I had pushed objectivity to the point where even orgasm paled beneath my glance. Or was I being merely pathological? I remembered Rudhyar's description of the fully evolved Scorpio, who is able 'even when the flame burns most intensely, to remember that he is merely the keeper of that flame, and is not to be consumed by it.' With a groan, romanticism died within me, and I felt an infinite pang at its demise through exposure.

The climax was, so to speak, anticlimactic.

And immediately afterwards I was disgusted with myself. I had done something wrong, following Hemingway's dictum that a moral act is one you feel good after. Then the despair hit, and I let everything go. For a brief instant I felt peacefully dead. At last and of course, this was what I had been dreading all my life, and desperately seeking: the quietness of the grave. And then I came out of it to the game-world, but refreshed, stronger, and clearer.

Then the trip began. It was as though we were tied to each other. We had no obvious reason to be with one another physically, but neither of us could stand to have the other out of sight for more than a few minutes. We couldn't sleep, for fear we would lose one another. When I had to leave to buy cigarettes, she came with me. We went for a walk through the East Village, where I kept a complete control over her, refusing to let her camp it up on the street. 'You're walking with me now,' I said, 'and you'd better behave. You're acting like you're doped. That's merely an affectation.' She looked at me with resentful admiration. Then I began to see her clearly, perceiving her essence and how her personality manifested itself around it. I saw all the history of her life and of her people. Once, when I had asked her why she felt doomed to self-destruction, she said: 'I made up my mind to make myself as happy as possible wherever I am, and I just let myself go where fate takes me. I *am* the Fates.'

'That's absurd,' I said. 'No, it's Jewish,' she answered, and in a stroke the entire psychic history of the Jews came glaring home in utter clarity. I looked at her again, this broken human being of twenty-one, scarred by her parents' private traumas and carrying the collective guilt of over four thousand years; this child with her stubborn ways and winning wiles; this woman who let herself be beaten and degraded, and yet through it all showed a heartbreaking warmth and delightful intelligence. She was at once a whore and a mother, a sprite and a fool, a lover and a murderer. She was, in short, a typical woman. The only difference was that she lived all her contradictions fully, accepted the irony of a dualistic version and learning to live in living paradox.

We ran into the East Village scene, that melange of pitiful humanity and engrossing metatheatre. At one spot we ran across an old man who had signs pinned to his shirt, reading: 'It's not Marxism, Christianity, or Astrology. Woman dominates.' On his ass he had a sign which said: 'Master of women.' Next to him was one of those faded, bearded, young-old men who prowl the streets of the Village digging everything with a sweet sadness and insight. The old man was saying, 'There's seven levels of women. Most men marry those from one to four. The seventh level has the real dominators. The movie actresses.' His example seemed misplaced, but the metaphysics interested me. I decided to question his acuity. 'What would you say she is?' I asked, pointing to

Carol. He appraised her with a glance and said, 'Oh, she's a five or six.' Instantly I knew he was right. 'Thanks,' I said. 'That's right on.' And I shook his hand and left.

We walked down second avenue, past Ratner's, that symbol of decaying Jewish gentility, still gallantly serving Old World food with European waiters to a new army of longhairs and odd types, all with perfect nonchalance and sophistication laced with a mammoth world-weariness. The black cats and Puerto Ricans watched Carol as she passed, her bare legs flashing under her short skirt. Her bra-less breasts jiggled as she walked, and her face had that vacant nodding look of the junkie. I remembered once before fucking she had said, 'Roll a joint. Give me a fix first, and then fuck me.' I flashed her five years from now, syphilitic and mindless, prey to whatever brutality wished to pluck her from her Opheliaesque trance to ravish her. I was witnessing the beginning stages of the total degradation of a human being.

I tried to talk to her, to make her see her life from this viewpoint, this very real possibility. But interpretations given too soon are not heard; their truth may be realised years later, but only when the person is ready for them. The rap went on despite all my intuition. We had moved from an acid high to a speed trip.

Rap rap rap rap rap. It sounds like someone knocking at the door, and that is what it is . . . words being machine-gunned at the door of the mind, attempting to splinter the wood and penetrate to the inside. But their own rapidity, and their blocking of all feedback, are the very reasons they do not register.

We ate at the Odessa, walked through Tompkins Square Park, and dug on the vivacity of the city, the mixing races and nationalities and ages. Raving tattered madmen standing next to dealers standing next to cops standing next to Ukrainian grandfathers who are watching innocent children playing in the grass. Oh, what a spectacle mankind was at that moment; its entire drama lay etched in the scene before my eyes.

We got back, still tied to each other, wanting to rip away, but we were on a strange energy level, and we talked for the next thirty-six hours. We read to one another from our favourite books; we played music from all ages and nations; we made mobiles from telephone wire; we took baths; we fucked; we began putting our cigarettes out on the floor; forgetting to eat, forgetting to look or listen, just caught up in the kaleidoscopic merry-go-round of our turbulent inner lives.

At the end of that time, I seemed suddenly to snap to. I looked up with all the surprise of a man coming out of unconsciousness and waking up in a strange room. I saw this nude body across the floor, and it was attached to a strange face. It was Carol, but stripped of all the images I had plastered on her during two weeks. I saw her as fresh as on the first night I met her, but now I saw with the eyes of experience made rich with the suffering of sharing her pain and joy. Tears rolled down my eyes, for I knew in an instant that I would have to leave her. I could not sustain what would be necessary to help her out of her morass. She would drag me into her youthful insanity.

I had learned much from her, and she from me. We had not abused one another. And the pain of seeing a dream disappear was compensated for by the warmth of remembering the life we had so intimately shared for a few brief weeks. I looked at her. 'I don't want to live with you,' I said. She began to say something, and then stopped herself. 'All right,' she said. And a light went out somewhere in the universe, and love covered its face in the veils of sorrow.

(13)

ALL UP AND down Third Avenue the casualties of our civilisation hobbled through their days, the pimps and whores, the bums and drunks, the violent blacks seeking prey, and the police who prowl the streets like game wardens in a preserve for dangerous animals. I looked down at them from my window and for a moment saw the entire thing as a scene from some grotesque drama. In one of the hallways a beautiful girl with a trim but full body stood waiting for a score. I felt a great distance from her, removed in time and space and affinity.

Then the thought of Carol disrupted my mind. She had left two days earlier, to crash with some friends who were part of the international gang of students and academic drifters which covers the globe like a thin web. I felt a great sorrow as she went, glad to have her troubles out of my immediate vicinity, but wondering whether she would be all right in this life. I wondered what it would be like to be passing Third Avenue one day and see Carol standing in a hallway like the girl across the street. The woman standing there now must have a man somewhere for whom she is special, for whom her body is sacred. Or maybe because she never knew such a man (or woman), she was able to treat her flesh as an item for the marketplace. I shuddered. In a flash the mask of whore dropped from her face and she was simply a person, like myself, like anyone, but now leaning against a building and ready to expose the deepest part of her body, the spot where love meets lust to produce life, to any gawking, leering, hard-staring creep who might pass by.

And what was there to be done? Children died daily of starvation and napalm. Entire peoples were enslaved. War machinery polluted the earth and a cloud of poison gas was accumulating over the entire planet. In some places, outright slavery still flourished, while everywhere one or another form of imperialism reduced most of mankind to mindless servitors. In the face of that, of what significance was a young whore peddling her pussy on Third Avenue?

In a flash, embodied in that girl, the whole of the pain of the species manifested itself. Unnatural, the human race had, as an organism, gone collectively insane. Trillions of dollars had been spent on armaments to protect us from one another, when all we need to do is to share what is available. The scene had become so bad that people were already splitting for the moon, bringing, of course, their poisons and filth with them.

It was very difficult to see Carol leave. In a very short time I had grown very close to her. Yet, as so often happens, the rush of intimacy moved too quickly and reversed itself, at which point we were left to confront one another as strangers. The last time we fucked summed up the complete relationship. In the dark moaning movement of our bodies and eyes, in the touch and dance of that most deep wordless communion, everything was clear. Yet when she walked out the door, her face flushed, her knit dress outlining the curves of her buttocks and the pert bulge of her nipples, the woman I had been with in bed seemed like a totally different creature. I saw myself as one of the thousands of men who might look at Carol as she walked down the street. I too would be captivated by the inviting ass, the lush breasts, the slightly sluttish gleam of her eyes. She would make a momentary impression, and I would pass by, forgetting her immediately.

How many thousands of women had I so coolly appraised, forgetting that each of them has all the potential for the deep groaning passion where all meaning lies? And what did it take to transform a woman from a visual object and focus of a sex fantasy to an actual woman, with all her pain and complexity and singing need? The first night I fucked Carol she was simply a piece of ass, and I revelled in the discoveries I made about her body. When I cupped my hand over her cunt and felt how wet and hot it was, my first thought was, 'Wow, I've got a live one!' And now, what would I think of any man who took Carol to bed and thought the same thing? The very idea of it makes me sick, and the contradiction clangs in my mind. Do I then despise myself? Given my obsessive nature, it would be awful to link up to it the need to suffer, and end with a compulsive masochism, a continual throwing of oneself into real and fantasy situations where it always comes up with blood in the teeth.

Now the jealousy began, and I prepared to do my penance, to pay for the sin of having enjoyed another human being sexually for two weeks. I began to imagine all the men she would fuck, the gang bangs, the rapes, the scenes of degradation. And in all of them, it was never the picture of her that bothered me, but the fact that her yielding, loving, wanting, and ultimately pure centre was being filthied by this army of superficial bandits, plundering her cunt for their mean pleasure. Again and again I tried to insert myself into their place, but I couldn't get away from the fact that by sending her away, I was condemning her to her fate, and I viewed with a brooding premonition what that fate might be.

Somehow it always returned to sex, the original sin, the means whereby we learn to differentiate good and evil and all the other dualities. Male and female face one another in eternal separation, striving to fuse, and dying in loneliness. Perhaps only those Japanese lovers who tie their bodies together and let themselves fall, embracing, from high cliffs onto a rocky shore: perhaps they know what ultimate union is. I have never trusted the mystics who claim to know unity with the Absolute as they sit on their asses in some posh cave, smiling to themselves. Union must be total, and that includes the flesh and blood and balls and cunt of the human being, not just his mind.

Now, after a lifetime of experience, after the bruising relationship with Regina, and the short, searing affair with Carol, I faced the same enigma. Why is it that the minute I begin having sex with someone, the quality of our relationship so radically changes as to make it a different kind of organism? Why, with sex, do freedom and respect and friendship so often go out the window? Why can I be happy for any woman's sexual freedom, and have that same joy turn into jealousy the minute she becomes 'my' woman? I had wracked my brain for years over this dilemma, and although I now had a wealth of experience to draw on, the problem was no closer to being solved. My only consolation was that I could now ask more acute questions.

Carol had come roaring into my life, a mixture of honest enthusiasm and a compulsion to run. Deflowered when she was four, subject to harsh beatings from her father, gifted with a joyous body and a sensitive clitoris, she had lived a Holly Golightly existence since she was sixteen. She could from moment to moment change from a hard, calculating bitch to a warm, efficient house-wife to a near-nymphomaniac who had orgasms in her sleep as she lay there moaning and pressing her thighs together, working out in her body some fancy fleeting through her mind. On a few nights I lay next to her, my cock hard and my stomach in knots as I watched her gyrate and cry out, crushing her cunt into itself, yearning for some phantom lover, the one who would penetrate her once and for all, who would offer her the final humiliation . . . the man who would kill her. For she wanted to die, to be sacrificed. She was for-ever being ripped off, and letting herself be used by men who are little better than swine in their sense of scope and honour.

And I had loved her at once, a loved laced with instantaneous fear of loss, for I sensed that she was a bird on the wing, following the wind to the north. For the first few days we fucked, I was still able to keep my centre, to hold onto my perspective. I could keep track of all the many selves she was, and not get lost in any single one of them. To have done so would have been to reinforce one image at the expense of all the others, and perhaps substitute that bolstered *persona* for the actual human being, who was always mysterious, always changing.

But when the fucking got really intense, when I started to know her as a person and not as a source for sensation, it became impossible for me to maintain a purely phenomenological outlook. In the beginning I could look upon her love of animals, say, and her proclivities towards prostitution as equal manifestations in her personality. But after having tasted the sweet juices of her cunt, after having heard her gasp with pleasure/pain as I bit her nipple, having felt the burning need in her surge to me looking for completion, I could not remain partial any longer. I became defensive of certain aspects of her; I didn't want her to go out into the street with her nipples showing; I didn't want other men raping her with their eyes.

As with everything, there were two aspects to my change in attitude. On the one hand I became more attentive, more loving, more involved in her. But simultaneously, I lost the ability to observe her dispassionately, and slowly became embroiled in her inner drama. What was worse, I began to get tangled in my own metatheatre, losing sight of my own costume changes and sly use of masks. Soon a confused man was floundering with a confused woman, and we lost all ability to make simple contact, to enjoy the simple perception and presence of one another.

With that came a feeling of panic, for when communication gets muddy, the individual gets paranoid. We would go to bed at night, with everything superficially fine, and no sooner did the lights go out than the monsters started oozing from the walls. We heard noises, imagined men with razor blades climbing in through the windows, felt the clammy presence of ghosts. Perhaps a dozen times I would leap from bed to storm into the next room, there to confront emptiness and silence where I had expected some form of enemy. And return to bed, shaken, to seek comfort in her arms. And the step from comfort to sex is not a very long one.

That was strange fucking, the fucking for reassurance. Neither of us would be especially turned on, but the newness of one another's bodies had not yet worn off, and the simple nearness and heat kicked off enough excitement to stir us. We would begin stroking one another lightly, with no more pressure than a feather might give. It was as though each of us were defining the outline of the other's body by coming only so close as to let the electrical fields around the bodies mingle. It was like combining auras.

There was no desire in this, except perhaps a desire for desire. We wanted and needed to fuck, but it was an intellectual concern, something to be done to satisfy one of the imperatives of the

264

mind. The heart was not involved, and the body was indifferent. Soon the stroking would have its inevitable effect: her cunt got wet and my cock got hard. She would slide her ass across the sheet towards me, in what is perhaps the sexiest gesture I have ever seen. The sight of her young white body, stirred and hesitant, coming towards me in order to make it easier to fuck her, is one that shall never leave the area of instant recall in my memory.

At that point it became a simple mechanico-chemical process. Her left leg goes up bringing the knee to her breast, her right leg stays extended, and her cunt opens in a maddening slant caused by the stretch of her legs in opposite directions. My cock goes for it like a kingfisher dives into a river for its victim. At first there is no great sensation, for she is not very excited. But the cock soon works its unfailing magic, and in a while she responds. The difference now is that she is not responding to me, but to the fucking that I am doing. We become quite impersonal, sealing our minds so as to keep our fantasies private from one another. There is no attempt to blend our minds and bodies into a double two-level synthesis which must take place if the hearts are to open. This kind of fucking is just her grunting her way through the levels of her tension to a cramped inverted orgasm, and me sailing blindly on the curve of my long-awaited ejaculation until the sperm in my balls grudgingly stirs itself to shoot up my cock, out, and into the grasping cunt.

At one point she got tangled in the blankets, and I pulled them back, involuntarily covering her face and torso with them. The ensuing sight inflamed me, and I continued fucking her like that, with just her legs exposed, thrusting into the anonymous cunt, picturing her as the archetypal slut accepting whatever meat was flung at her. Then she threw the blankets off and turned her back to me. I fucked her from behind as we both lay on our sides, and when that didn't get to the place I wanted to be, I turned her over on her belly. Immediately the act changed. She lifted her ass and I plunged very deep inside her. I brought my knees to the backs of her knees and urged her legs forward. She crawled up and then came to a kneeling position, her ass high and cunt hanging down totally open and exposed. Her shoulders were hunched and her head lay at an angle to the horizontal of her torso. Her eyes were open and vacant, and with one hand she gently stroked my hand as it pressed onto the mattress, supporting my arm and my entire torso. The delicate movements of her fingers were like those of a child stroking a baby rabbit. I saw the child that was still alive in her, that aspect which only emerges as a kind of stubborness in her social role, but which blossoms in all its fragility when she is being fucked. And right upon that came the notion of her as a whore, lying in her bed, waiting for the stranger to enter. I am the stranger. I find this young and fleshy woman-child lying there, nude and uninterested. I begin to fuck her and she dutifully offers me her cunt. But halfway through, the flame stirs inside her, and she begins to give parts of herself that she would want to be seen by, want to share with, only those men that she knows long and well, who will be able to appreciate the deep, rich beauty of her. But I, as the client, am brutal, and all I can do is to take a gleeful excitement in the fact that this whore is enjoying being fucked, indeed, wants only to be fucked, and can lie there exposing not only her hole but her inner life, as her tender cunt is blasted again and again by a demented cock.

I came up off my knees and supported myself only on my toes. This made it harder to bear the weight, but it gave me a very strong spring to my legs, so I was really able to launch myself into her. She felt the difference at once, and her mouth dropped open. It was as though she became rigid outside in order not to let any movement of hers distract from the hot deep penetration inside her. This was not fucking, this was civilised brutality. This was the male discharging all his hatred, using his strength to punish, to humiliate. This was woman in her role of vessel, accepting and nullifying the blast of using herself as a cushion, as a sponge, and while at it feeling those sensations and emotions which are only possible when one relaxes even in the face of sadism, and takes what comes.

All that came was me. I dragged the sperm up by sheer force of will, commanding it with the violent suction created in her cunt by my plunging in and out of her. She pushed back and took my bucking organ deep inside her, wriggling her ass so that the back of her pussy rubbed back and forth across the head of my cock as it spurted sperm into her. We froze like that for a long while, my pubis glued to her cunt and ass. And then, slowly, we sank onto the bed.

It was not long after that that she left. It was a chilly May day, and she was wearing the knit dress and white raincoat which had become a kind of costume for her. I remembered the first night I met her, when she was decked out like the Madwoman of Chaillot. She was so much wilder then, so much more actively crazy. In two short weeks, after the intensity of what we shared, she had become quieter, closer to herself. It was but a glimpse of the astounding woman she could be, once the fear and insecurity of being without a man to love left her. 'I'm just a very old-fashioned girl,' she had said a number of times. 'I just want to get married and have babies and make a home.' And I believed that, for I have come to believe that unless a person is a true *sanyassi*, a wanderer, then a nest is necessary for sanity and survival, and the nest must be an organic unit in harmony with the countryside in which it is placed. ,

Part of my sorrow at letting her go was based on the idea that if we stayed together, I could help her undergo the sea-change so necessary to bringing all her pain and repressed memories to the surface, and letting them be burned off by a hot sunlight. But that would be playing therapist, a game I enjoyed when I was younger, but was always hurt by. Human destiny must be allowed to evolve, and any tampering is the most serious act. I did not have the strength or resolution to undertake to shape her life. I wondered if she would quickly revert to the role she seemed to need to keep her self-esteem. Would she become the professional scatterbrain, with all her genuine gestures spoiled simply because she held on to them a few seconds after the impulse had died, giving her an air of coy affectation? I knew enough of life to know that the most trivial behavioural quirk can change the course of a person's development and fortune, often even more so than major influences like education and breeding.

I walked downstairs with her. A taxi came. She asked me whether I had all the addresses she gave me. We would keep in touch. Perhaps San Francisco together in the fall . . .

I watched the back of the taxi until it was lost in distance and traffic. Then I went back upstairs, where the emptiness of the house assailed me. She was gone. I had accomplished what I wanted and felt like a successful engineer. But with the craziness, uncertainty, and fear, I had thrown out the warmth, the melting, the joy. I had disposed of a human being from my life. It is the kind of thing we have come to do casually with acquaintances and one-night lovers. And yet, and yet . . . as precious as I.

I went into the bedroom; the sheets were still rumpled and stained with our secretions. She was gone. I lay on the bed and felt the awful absence of her. A great burning began in my chest, and my limbs grew heavy. I felt like a lost child, and my lips trembled, and out of my pain-filled eyes I cried and I cried, weeping for all the loss that every human being is condemned to suffer in this brief stretch of breathing on this lovely, and dying, planet.